FALLEN EAGLES

FALLEN EAGLES

SIXTEEN 'RITES OF PASSAGE'
SHORT STORIES

BRUCE HARRIS

IN AID OF THE HUNTINGTON'S DISEASE
YOUTH ORGANISATION

The Book Guild Ltd

First published in Great Britain in 2021 by
The Book Guild Ltd
9 Priory Business Park
Wistow Road, Kibworth
Leicestershire, LE8 0RX
Freephone: 0800 999 2982
www.bookguild.co.uk
Email: info@bookguild.co.uk
Twitter: @bookguild

Copyright © 2021 Bruce Harris

The right of Bruce Harris to be identified as the author of this
work has been asserted by him in accordance with the
Copyright, Design and Patents Act 1988.

All rights reserved. No part of this publication may be
reproduced, transmitted, or stored in a retrieval system, in any form or by any means,
without permission in writing from the publisher, nor be otherwise circulated in
any form of binding or cover other than that in which it is published and without
a similar condition being imposed on the subsequent purchaser.

This work is entirely fictitious and bears no resemblance to any persons living or dead.

Typeset in 11pt Adobe Garamond Pro

Printed and bound in the UK by TJ Books Lmited, Padstow, Cornwall

ISBN 978 1913551 391

British Library Cataloguing in Publication Data.
A catalogue record for this book is available from the British Library.

To all patients, carers and staff associated with the Huntington's Disease Youth Organisation, and all the researchers in the U.K. and the rest of the world who are continuing their brave and unremitting endeavour to make the illness a thing of the past.

CONTENTS

FOREWORD	IX
FALLEN EAGLES	1
PICTURES OF PAULA	24
MAKING THE GRADES	33
THE BARD OF BROOKVALE	47
BEING DESDEMONA	60
YEARNING TO BREATHE FREE	66
WORD OF MOUTH	84
PLANES OF PAPER, DREAMS OF SMOKE	91
JENNIFER'S ROOM	106
HIGH TIDE	115
HOUR OF THE WOLF	122
THE LAMPEDUSA PASSAGE	136
FIRST NIGHT	148
MILLIE ELLIOT – LEARNING THE DRILL	155
THE HIGH DIVE	165
PARIS BY NIGHT	172

FOREWORD

HUNTINGTON'S DISEASE YOUTH ORGANISATION EN.HDYO.ORG

Huntington's Disease Youth Organization, HDYO, was set up in 2012 by a group of young people. Our goal is to provide support and education for young people (up to age 35 years) impacted by HD globally. We do this through providing professional support online, creating needed educational content for all age groups (kids, teens, young adults, parents and professionals), making our website and content available in as many languages as we can, connecting young people with their peers, making events such as youth camps and conferences around the world, motivating and providing opportunities for young people to get involved through volunteering and research and working with other HD organizations to improve what they offer young people also.

Additionally, our goal is to do our part as an organization to assist our research partners about the needs of young people. We hope that our collaboration with these partners will help speed up the process to bring needed medication to those with HD, around the whole world.

Huntington's Disease is a rare genetic neurogenerative condition that is cause by an expanded gene in a person's DNA. Huntington's is a condition which affects the nervous system and gradually gets worse over time. This means the condition affects the cells of our brains and continues to cause damage as time progresses which stops the brain and body from working as well as they used to. As a result, people develop symptoms of Huntington's disease. These symptoms can be divided into three main types: involuntary movements, cognitive and behavioural. Any child of a person who has the expanded gene that caused Huntington's Disease has a 50% chance of inheriting the expansion too.

The theme of Fallen Eagles aligns directly with young people impacted by Huntington's Disease. Their journey with disease takes them through many twists and turns but their decision to go through genetic pre-diagnostic testing for Huntington's disease is one of the biggest and scariest points in their lives. A young person at risk of Huntington's disease has to wait until they turn 18 before they can legally decide to test for Huntington's disease; this is their rite of passage. The testing and counselling process is long and tough, the implications of test reach beyond just carrying the gene. The consequences of testing for Huntington's disease have implications on career paths, ability to access financial products; such as insurance; future and current relationships, planning a family as well as their own health. They are carrying the knowledge that they will develop this condition that will rob them of every part of themselves, their mood, their movements and their memories.

Our work is only possible through the generous donations of our supporters like Fallen Eagle author Bruce Harris. Young people and their families impacted by Huntington's disease live in an endless cycle of grief and loss but through education, awareness and support we can help reduce isolation and help connect families with clinicians and researchers to ensure that as a collective group we are all part of ending this disease.

Cat Martin
Executive Director

FALLEN EAGLES

I was looking up so vertically that my neck strained to continue. Most of my view consisted of inaccessible black and brown rock, unforgiving, hard and sometimes sharp. But at the top, in silhouette, was the head and torso of a man, unmoving and unhurried, as my father always was. For him, the whole proposition was simple enough; he held the rope, his chip off the old block climber son was making his routine way up what he called the 'apprentice slopes' to be with him, and then we could sit triumphantly there, the summit achieved, masculinity fanfared, another solid brick laid in the foundation of my confidence.

I already knew how to freeze my terror. He didn't frighten me, my father, not in the conventional ways still quite usual in 1976; he had never laid an angry finger on me, he'd never come in drunk – none of that. But he was Dougal Murray, mountaineer, CBE medalled in his mid-thirties; I'd stood outside Buckingham Palace with him, watching that still, self-effacing but utterly self-confident smile of his. He'd held the award up, a big shiny thing with a ribbon, and they'd spent about thirty seconds snapping away at him before moving on to the next medalled celebrity. I'd been fourteen at the time, mute and little, bursting with pride but also aware of a cold douche of fear that I, his son Duncan, was no match for him and never would be.

We were about four hundred feet up, a climb which, for him, was weekend recreation. By this time, the endless summer of '76, I was sixteen, and my remorseless plod in his footsteps continued. I heard his words like hard and fast rules in a little well-remembered rule book – 'you are in charge, Duncan, your moods, your emotions, are entirely what you decide they will be. You don't need to look down, or around; if it's unsettling, if it breeds fear, you can just not do it. Your will is everything; your discipline is absolute. If you want it to be'.

We were on one of the Scottish munros, the classified climbs of Scotland; he thought if I really had it in mind to carry on where he, sooner or later, would leave off, making my way up some challenging lower portions of a few munros would be the best way to start. Some of them could almost be walked up, even though walking is an inadequate way to describe a head bent against wind and rain while at the same time watching where the feet are very carefully indeed, in the knowledge that a few loose stones could set them and you off on a rapid descent which might well break a bone or two, or worse. He wasn't coming out with any fatuous words of encouragement; he'd decided, I know, to start trying to treat me as a fellow climber, boy as I was. Instead of congratulating myself on living up to expectations, I was vaguely ashamed of perpetuating something of a con trick; I knew, or thought I knew, that my success in hiding my gut-turning fear was just another form of fear, fear of him, not of his displeasure or his punishment, but of disappointing him, becoming the inadequate little pup who somehow happened to be his son.

There was something in the stillness of his dark head above me which spoke of a restrained impatience, a resigned tolerance, which kicked at an emotion in me. I could see a foothold, dark and indistinct as it was, and my right foot lifted determinedly to it, almost of its own volition. At exactly the same moment, some enormous presence whooshed past only yards from my back; I edged away, lost my footing and suddenly I was hanging in fresh air, held on by a waist harness, as Scotland whirled around me, a long blue river snaking away into the distance, and within seconds, doing the same thing again. The harness strained against me, and a wild dizziness told hold, almost causing me to vomit; for one excruciating moment, I saw myself plunging downwards, and even at this modest height, the damage could be severe or even fatal. Apart from the harness, I had nothing on but boots, shorts and socks, and ridiculous as it was to imagine that more clothes would change anything, bareness accentuated vulnerability in my mind. And nothing, it seemed, stemmed the dizzy, whirling head and the torrent of sweat which must, by now, be obvious enough to my companions.

Gasping and swearing under my breath, I finally regained enough control to get my foot back on the hold I'd seen, and five scrambling minutes later I had joined my father and his brother cum-gamekeeper cum-personal assistant Uncle Stuart on the summit, or at least the point a quarter of the way up the mountain which was my apprentice climbing that day.

'Well done, lad', my father said, and it wasn't ruffled hair or patted cheek, all the child stuff, it was a touch on the hand and away, like he did with Uncle Stuart when they'd completed another routine conquest. Stuart himself, as always, wore a non-committal, slightly contemptuous expression and 'held his peace', as my father described what I saw as my uncle's politic silences. Uncle Stuart had been divorced for two years then, and everyone professed incredulity at the intransigence of my now former aunt, but Stuart was a dour, withdrawn, disapproving presence even with me, his oldest nephew, still young enough to want to get on with everyone, especially his relatives.

As usual, my relief and sense of accomplishment took over, for the time being at least, from my nausea at the height and breadth of where we were, the Cairngorms stretching away on all sides of us as far as the eye could see. Then I saw what had whooshed past me, a great giant of a golden eagle, as close as I had ever seen one, and a thrill in itself, with its huge wing span fully extended.

'There you are, son', my father said. 'We're even higher than the eagles today. How will that do you?'

'He's hovering for a kill', Uncle Stuart said, in the deflating way he had. 'Or he's after bringing in the big girl. That's why he's so low'.

'Yes, sure enough, Stuart', said my father. 'But he's a sight for sore eyes, for all that'.

And so he was, a beautiful, smoothly turning vision against the vast mingled blue/grey sky. And, of course, Uncle Stuart was right, as he tended to be when some dismal outcome was in prospect. Female golden eagles are larger than males, and we only had to look a short distance to the right to see our eagle's arriving mate, the generous feathers of her great wings ruffling in the wind and her talons already out. The male eagle swooped downwards in an enormous, graceful curve, and almost immediately under the zenith of his arc, as if he was using himself as a downward arrow, were two forlorn figures, a ewe and a young lamb detached from the main flock, perhaps disorientated in the unfamiliar heat. Although it was July, the lamb looked no more than five or six weeks old; lambing happens when the weather changes for the better, and in the Highlands, that can take time.

The female acted on cue immediately, diving with gathering violence down upon the sheep, its great talons sinking deeply into the back of the lamb. By the time the ewe had rallied itself from its panic, the lamb was off, head dangling, the birds coming closer to each other as if in self-congratulation and heading off eastwards. Within seconds, the lamb's body had stilled until it was no more than a little white sack with legs. Below, the ewe did a kind of revolving walk, bleating piteously towards nothing in particular.

My father shook his head slowly in the philosophical way he had; Uncle Stuart's eyes had narrowed, almost in admiration. They were not men for homilies or platitudes, and Stuart went straight to the practicalities.

'That's on Ian Lessiter's land. If he ever sees them at it, he'll shoot the pair of them'.

'That should be against the law', I said.

'Huh'. Uncle Stuart was up on his feet, ready to go. 'Fat lot Lessiter would care about that. It's his livestock they're away with'.

'Right enough, boys', my father said, and my uncle's eyes narrowed again at this lumping him together with me. 'What comes up needs to go down, and I'm ready for a wee drink'.

Two years on, and running, not climbing, occupied most of my fitness time, thanks to my father managing to track down the root cause of my terror at even modest heights. Absurdly, it wasn't on a climb that the sudden revelation came, it was on a balcony in an Alpine hotel, not long before I was to attempt my most ambitious effort yet on a real Alpine mountain. I was seventeen then, and still steeling myself to stay in control of my balance and emotions. I knew my climbing had become a source of contention between my parents; my mother was convinced that I suffered from some form of vertigo, for some reason as yet unknown, but it certainly wasn't that I was overweight and it could hardly be a lack of fitness.

Dad was showing me the ridiculously beautiful snow-bound view from the hotel window; he'd stepped out on to the balcony to get the full advantage of it. As I started to follow him, the room and the view began to revolve around me; I clutched on to a door handle, and that noise made him turn. I suppose my appearance gave him the clue he needed. Before mountaineering more or less took over his life, in courses, rescue teams, lectures, tours etc., he had been a doctor, and once he was on to the signals, it all progressed quite quickly.

We sat one evening in the conservatory at the back of the house, the glorious Scottish highland countryside descending before us, and no more than quarter of a mile away, our own private loch, Loch Murray we called it; strictly speaking, it was hardly big enough to qualify as a loch, but it was much larger than the average swimming pool and served as one when the weather allowed or we felt tough enough.

'Your mother was right, Duncan', he said. 'As she is wont to be. You have something called Meniere's Disease. It's a condition of the inner ear which affects balance and hearing. Annoyingly, it's one of those conditions where no-one knows the exact cause, though there are heavy suggestions of genetic connections, and one of your mother's brothers, your Uncle Peter, has suffered from vertigo since childhood, which is what made your mother suspicious in the first place; we may have a connection there'.

I glanced across at him. I'd been permitted to join him occasionally in his single alcoholic indulgence; he drank good wine sometimes, if sparingly. There were no other alcoholic drinks he had any time for, and if anyone brought anything in that line on one of his climbs, they were likely to suffer for it. I saw him in profile, when, to me, his formidable character was even more evident than full on facial; the firm, very defined slightly stubbled chin, the long nose, the deep brown eyes that spoke of both strength and intelligence.

Before I'd put together some kind of response, he turned full on to me, and his eyes were as warm as I'd ever seen them.

'The condition is likely to deteriorate as you get older, Duncan, and much as it goes against the grain, I suspect for both of us, you will have to stop climbing now. But what I would say, son, is the efforts you've made in that direction are a testimony to your guts and determination, and you shouldn't, you mustn't, think any less of yourself because you cannot climb, because I certainly won't'.

He raised his glass towards me, and through slightly misted eyes, I understood that this was now the grown-up thing which would happen between us, and I raised mine accordingly.

And so I took to fell running, every bit as challenging in its own way, and just as capable of preserving the fitness which was regarded as basic to life in my family. By the time I was eighteen and on the verge of university, my brother James, aged sixteen, had replaced me as the potential climbing heir, and Uncle Stuart's daughter Alison, aged fifteen, had already started 'nursery sloping'.

Uncle Stuart himself, of course, remained unconvinced about my condition. Never in my life had he articulated any thoughts concerning my general wimpishness, and perhaps it was adolescent over-sensitivity on my part attributing thoughts to him which he didn't have, but his taciturn and sometimes even snappy attitudes towards me made my interpretation credible enough. There was also a visible difference in his attitudes towards me and my brother that he didn't appear to make any attempt to conceal. James would usually get something along the lines of 'now then, young man' and the expression which passed as a smile for Uncle Stuart; at least that's what I took it to be, as I'd had precious little sight of it myself. As my eighteenth birthday passed, I deliberately dropped the 'uncle' and started calling him 'Stuart'. The first couple of times produced angry glares, but then he settled to it with a kind of 'well, what can you expect?' attitude, and James became ever more the blue-eyed boy. James didn't confess himself exactly exhilarated. He already had a dry, laconic humour all of his own. 'Well, aren't I just the lucky one', he said, and rolled his eyes. James had and has the ability to make me laugh out loud, and I think he enjoys doing so.

One of my final runs, in early September shortly before I was to set off for what looked like a whole new life at Durham University, became a revelation in both good and bad ways. The great advantage of running compared with climbing is that it allowed me to think, rather than having to concentrate my entire being on controlling my terror. Watching my feet pounding as best they could through a particularly wet and rocky patch, it suddenly dawned on me very forcefully that I was my mother's son more than my father's. My mother made her living as a journalist; I aspired to be a writer, as did so many millions of others, and my mother was one of the tiny percentage of us who did actually make a living out of it. It was on one of my father's climbs that they'd met, in the hotel where they were both staying, my mother working on one of her travel pieces and finding herself intrigued by this mountaineering man that everyone seemed to know, though the mountaineering man was all of twenty-two years old at that time, the same age as she was. In one of his rare but gratifying expansive moments, my father described his first sight of her.

'She was in the bay window of the hotel bar, looking out over the view, as spectacular as Scotland can do. There was a sunset, Duncan, and part of the light of it was catching the side of her face, such an unblemished, wonderful face, and her long hair, oh that long free hair of hers, sweeping down to her shoulders. She was entranced by Scotland, and I was entranced by her. Her head turned towards me, and I know people call it a cliché, an apocryphal thing which never really happens, but it did. It really did. We knew'.

From an early age, I noticed heads, usually mostly male, turn to look whenever she made an entrance, the one and only Mary Murray nee Sutherland, and it made James and I proud to see them together, especially when Dad was in his dinner suit, suave, tanned, sparkling-eyed, acting as a suitable consort to this stunning woman, whose sense of dress was as superb as her natural beauty.

As for my natural beauty, I can't say I'd noticed, although more than once, people, usually Sutherland relatives, had commented that I looked more like my mother than my father. In the way of Scottish boys of the time, I suppose, my first inclination was to take offence, or at least adopt the dour neutrality of indifference to adult remarks of this kind which tends to characterise boyhood. 'Mummy's boy' was still used widely as an insult at the time. It took me until I was eighteen, sitting not very comfortably on a rock in the Scottish countryside half way through my daily run, to realise that, regardless of physical appearance, my writing ability, such as it was, came from my mother. Dad did write occasionally, for course material, reports, etc., but while I aspired to write creatively, she did it, and while my largest audience to date was the few hundred who read the school magazine, her constant and loyal following ran into thousands and thousands. Her family might have kindly donated their Meniere's Disease to me, but she had given me a precious gift way beyond that, and if she'd given me good looks as well, why should there be anything wrong with that?

Thoughts chased themselves around in my head as I sat on that rock. The rain started pattering down and I got up and re-started; I knew just how far and how fast the rain came down in these parts, and while I'd been soaked often enough before, my train of thought was taking me to interesting places which the climate was not going to blot out if I could avoid it.

The effort of running while getting progressively wetter darkened my mood, and as usual when this happened, my thoughts moved reluctantly in the direction of my Uncle Stuart. One of the main sources of my resentment towards him, I realised, was the way he puppy-dogged around – there was no other way of putting it – my mother. Rumours abounded that one of the reasons why he'd broken with my ex-aunt Anne, who'd always seemed a pleasant and attractive enough woman to me, was because of his 'way with the ladies', people said quietly, in their euphemistic Scottish way. His way with my mother, fawning, praising, fetching and carrying when she wanted, and sometimes even when she didn't, seemed to largely amuse my father, but it didn't me, and perhaps it was this tendency of mine which had turned him against me. Boys always think they're being clever enough not to show their real agenda, but it's rarely true. And I had to confess, while the rain slowly turned me into a kind of mobile rag, that her apparent reciprocation at times didn't please me very much either, this beautiful woman who must have become well accustomed to choking off unwanted attentions from men, smiling unnecessarily broadly at him, sharing his little jokes, even the more risque ones, and sometimes even in my father's presence, amused as he claimed he was. Alright, Stuart had a mountaineering reputation himself – 'the redoubtable Murray brothers', I remember one headline calling them – but he was not to be compared to my father; he was smaller, uglier – to me, at least – and with a good deal less charm.

Eventually, I approached the house, looking forward to getting out of my dripping clothes and into a hot bath, but even the rain could not stop me from being arrested in my tracks by the sight I saw in our main living room at the front of the house. The light was fading, and perhaps because they wouldn't have been able to see much from the window anyway, my mother and Stuart were apparently engrossed in each other. She was at her writing bureau, as she called it, and he was leaning over her on her right; one hand was on her back, and the other was almost holding her hand. She had turned her face towards him; their heads were much too close together. His head went back and he laughed heartily, something I had never seen him do in my presence, and as he left her, moving towards the curtains, his hand again touched her back.

As he moved towards the window, I began running again, and he was closing the last curtain as I clattered up to the front door. My eyes daggered at him, emphatically enough for him to pause and step back, but then he smiled his more usual contemptuous little grimace and the curtain came rapidly across to shut me away.

Three years on, and the day forever seared into my consciousness like a branding. Wednesday November 18th 1981, not long after the start of my third and final university year, and on my way to a reputable English degree, according to my tutors, anyway. University halls were well behind me, and I was in a house share with three other students in Church Street, Durham. My room upstairs had an impressive view of the Cathedral. All of my trepidations about giving myself over voluntarily into the clutches of the English had proved unfounded. There were other Scots at Durham, of course; it took students from all over the world, but my three house mates were two Englishmen and a Canadian. It was a decent-sized house, for a terrace, and we all had rooms of our own. Sometimes I missed the wide open spaces of the Highlands, but I went back there during holidays and County Durham offered both countryside and coastline in abundance.

I had been to the athletics club for a training night; I was tired and a bit dispirited by the November gloom. Even at twenty one years old and in the peak of fitness, the training run had been demanding; keeping both the fitness side and the degree revision afloat was not easy. As I walked up to the house, it seemed to be unusually quiet and sombre; at times, I could hear the cheerful rattle of the lads from half way down the street.

This impression was confirmed as soon as I entered the front door. The television was on, in the main living room on my left as I went in. In the room itself, my three house mates were all standing, almost as if in respectful tribute. They only seemed to hear me when I whammed my bag down on a chair just inside the door. The Canadian guy, Brad Deanes, as easy going a lad as you can imagine, turned his face to me and it was pale.

'Oh, God', he said. 'Duncan – buddy –'

The other two turned together, and my closest friend here, Mike Wellfield, moved towards me and started to say something, but he didn't seem able to get the words out.

'What is it, boys? What's happening –' I said, just before the words on the televison started to seep into my weary brain.

'It is thought Mr. Murray's fall was the result of a faulty harness; there is little else that could explain such a catastrophic accident happening to such an experienced climber. Dougal Murray had climbed almost every challenging mountain in the world without incident; this Himalayan fall, of some 8000 feet, was both his first and his last'.

I stood aghast, feeling as if I'd passed through a portal into some ghastly parallel universe. They even had footage, from a distance, of the medics and fellow climbers gathered around my fallen father. An awful feeling came over me that next they would actually be taking a camera in to look at his broken body.

Whether I should have been exhibiting some stiff necked Scottish self-control or not, I didn't know, or care. I was down on my knees, and preparing myself to howl my head off like a beaten dog, when the phone suddenly rang. Brad went to answer it, and came back seconds later, looking even paler.

'Duncan, it's your uncle. Are you sure –'

I got up, strolled into the hall and grabbed the phone.

'Duncan, terrible news, I'm afraid – ', Stuart started saying, in that so matter-of-fact voice of his, which infuriated me even more than it usually did.

'Yes, Stuart, I know. I'm watching it on the news', I said, calmly enough, but with an emphatic and deliberate sarcasm on the last five words. Something inside me screamed crazily through my whole system that this man, who spends half his life with my father, has not managed to get a single word to me until I'm watching a public news bulletin. I was about to unleash a whole broadside of obscenities at him before, for the first very conscious time but by no means the last, some force, some entity, outside me made my stay my hand.

'I know it's not easy for you either, Uncle, but could you

not have got some word of this to me before now, or organised someone else to do it? Honestly?'

'I'm sorry, boy, O.K.?' That 'boy' again. 'This is the Himalayas – smooth communications are impossible –'

He kept talking, but I didn't hear him anymore, because at that moment, bursting through the front door using the key I'd given her, was my girlfriend already becoming more than a girlfriend, Josephine Reynolds, known to all the world except her parents as Josie.

'I'll talk with you later, Uncle', I said to the phone, and the next instant I was on Josie's slim shoulder, her arms were around me, and I was crying like a big, heart-broken baby. She exchanged a few words with the boys, which I can't remember, and then we went up to my room and I cried myself dry. She got hold of a brandy from somewhere and eventually, we just sat on the bed looking over Durham towards the cathedral. Maybe someone over there or in there could make sense of this, I thought, because I couldn't.

The next six months remain mostly a blur. I got through it, with the help of Josie, James and several others, in so far as I survived and kept myself on course for some kind of a degree, but nothing could be the same, I knew, and as the weeks went by, my mood darkened more and more. I could see it, and I knew those around me could see it as well, but there seemed no way to stop it happening, the growing cancer of suspicion and distrust within me.

Dad had told me on more than one occasion when the subject of his safety came up, as it obviously will for anyone who spends a lot of time climbing mountains, that he and Stuart had a regular routine which involved thoroughly checking each other's equipment, including the harnesses, before setting off on any climb. Since they were such experienced and respected climbers, I doubted anyone else would be involved. So if Dad had, for once, checked his equipment and missed something, might Stuart had made some decision about not picking up on it?

Every time my thoughts turned in this direction, I would dismiss it as being absurd; my father and uncle were devoted to each other and always had been. But, also every time, that scene I saw as I returned from my run would come back to haunt me – his hands, his face, her apparent acquiescence – and the time it took me to dismiss the idea as absurd became longer and longer, until I reached the point of recognising that I no longer saw it as being absurd at all. My uncle was in love with my mother, so strongly that even doing away with his own brother had to happen to clear his path.

I will always remember 1982 with a shudder. As it went on, I felt myself to be in something like a trance, going through the motions – the funeral procession, with hundreds lining the street, the media tributes, from some famous people I didn't even know my father knew, my drunken binge nights on the town with James, trying to get into punch-ups and occasionally succeeding, my frantic, over-energetic love-making with Josie which sometimes alarmed and worried her – all drifted by in a kind of blur. Even Stuart's stricken face at the funeral didn't allay my suspicions, and the very physical way he and my mother were consoling each other didn't either.

Then, as I was readying myself to leave the University in late June, with exams over and results to come, the blow fell. My morale was low to begin with; Josie's patience was at last wearing thin, I was not expecting anything more than a mediocre degree, 2.2. at best, and that probably wouldn't help too much in getting the job which had so far eluded me. Yes, I could work in the family business, as James dryly described it, making a shrine and a museum to my father, as well as continuing the courses and catering for them. But being permanently in the company of my mother and Stuart was more than I could stomach.

A long letter arrived from my mother, written in the style she used when she wanted to persuade me of something she knew I wouldn't like very much, cajoling, almost pleading at times, with a little judicious flattery thrown in.

'I think the remaining family does need to be together now, darling, and James is being difficult about that, but he has always looked up to you, and rightly so, of course, and if you were able to come home and stay home for a while, it may also bring him back. No-one and nothing can replace your father, we both know that, but that's all the more reason why we need to come together. I should tell you, Duncan, because there will be no secrets between us, that your uncle and I have made an unofficial engagement arrangement, with a view to marrying sometime next year, so as to not be too close to the loss of your father. I am too vulnerable now to go on alone, darling; your uncle is not your father, but he is the closest I have, I have known him as long as I've known your father, and starting again with someone entirely new would be too much for me, as would remaining a mourning widow for the rest of my life. Please try to be understanding, Duncan; I am still a relatively young woman and I knew your father well enough to know he would want me to find happiness with someone else if I could; in fact, he said as much to me on more than one occasion. In his profession, it is something we did need to talk about from time to time'.

Yes, I thought, trying not to crumple the paper in my hand, but whether or not he had Stuart in mind I doubt. She went on, pages and pages of it, attempting to appease me after dropping that thunderbolt into my life, and all she succeeded in doing was to confirm my every suspicion, once again with that scene in my mind, standing in the near-dark, wet and cold, while she and Stuart got it together.

I knew people who were staying in Durham for the summer, either because they rented all the year round or because they had fixed themselves up summer jobs, so I teamed up with a house share and got hold of a bar job in the city. Letters flew between my mother and I, long and plaintive on her part, brief and evasive on mine – I needed to earn money until I had a good job, I'd taken a liking to Durham etc. Josie was going home to her family on the coast at Scarborough, and I promised to go and see her when the opportunity arose, but by then there were tensions between us; this sullen, taciturn boy, racked by suspicion and resentment, was not the one she had originally known and she was a girl, not a saint.

It was in September when the real evil grew in me. The Scottish shooting season starts on September 1st, and one of the biggest in our area was on the Lessiter estate, which did holiday accommodation and well-organised shoots, the main one in October, when the pheasants were in season as well as everything else. When the golden eagle carried a lamb away from the farm part of the Lessiter estate and my uncle predicted that Ian Lessiter would shoot it if he saw it, I had no problem believing him; Lessiter was an ex-military man and a crack shot. His shoot also had an admired range of guns available for their guests.

I had no doubt that Stuart would be going to the Lessiter shoot. Apart from neighbourly duties, he was keen on shooting, as was my father, if not quite as much, and my father had less time to spare. I used to shoot myself, in the days when everything my father did I had to do, so my confidence in my ability just served to feed the plot my fevered mind was concocting. I made myself believe that Uncle Stuart was a cancer in my family who had plotted to dispose of my father, his very own brother, in order to claim my mother in marriage. Predictably, my father's will had left everything to my mother, meaning Stuart had not only stepped into my father's matrimonial shoes, he had also effectively disinherited his sons. I planned to dispose of Uncle Stuart with the same kind of well-planned apparent accident he had used to kill my father. Everyone would mourn again, complaining of the viciousness of fate, the injustice of events, but my family would be free of Stuart and able to take our future back into our own hands.

The most immediate problem was the interim period, when I would have to find some way of at least appearing to come to terms with the family situation. I wrote to my mother, one of the most careful and thought about pieces of writing I'd ever done, and even then, I'd done a few. The tone was that of the son accepting the inevitable, and I got it down, even if I was gritting my teeth as I wrote it.

'Nothing can bring Dad back now, and I'm sure he wouldn't want those of us who remain to spend the rest of our lives at each other's throats. I cannot promise that it will be easy for me, but I will come home and stay for the length of the shoot and perhaps a few days afterwards. The shoot will mean friends and neighbours will be about and we can cover the initial awkwardness with socialising and allowing people to sympathise and console'.

She wrote back a long letter so full of warmth and affection that I almost abandoned the whole plan. But that scene on the television, which had been so amplified and clarified by several documentaries since, of medical teams gathered around my poor father, came back to haunt me again, and at last I looked straight into the face of the real demon inside me. This wasn't about rescuing my family's future, this was no Machiavellian plot to save the Murrays. Vengeance is what I wanted, cold, hard vengeance, to answer the devil with the devil's own works.

On Wednesday October 14th, I went home in readiness for the shoot at the weekend. My mother received me with a long embrace as if a prodigal son had returned; Uncle Stuart grasped my hand as if he wanted to wrench it off and gave me his grimace of a smile. I was debriefed on 'the plans', as in the wedding scheduled for the summer of 1983, and I think I managed to look interested, though my mother looked unconvinced.

On Thursday morning, before we were due to set off for the Lessiter estate in the afternoon, I went for a run, for old times' sake, and to clear my head for what I had now convinced myself I had to do in my father's name, tough and bloody as it was. My mood caused me to take little notice of how far or where I was going, and eventually I realised I had almost run myself on to Lessiter land. Not far in the distance was the same munro I'd quarter-climbed with my father and Stuart at the age of sixteen, and that terrifying swing about in the Highland air came back to me in all its intensity. A glimmer of sense lingering around my embittered mind suggested I was now putting myself into the same kind of lost and dangerous position again, and then I saw a sight which stopped me, literally, in my tracks.

A golden eagle, a big, female golden eagle, was draped indecorously across two rocks, with so many pellet holes in her she could almost have been shot down by a machine gun. Her long graceful head was hanging backwards like a broken toy, and the blood, bones and feathers of what must have been her long death agony were spread all about her.

I sat down on a rock nearby and found myself unable to prevent the tears coming. Yes, the eagle was a lamb killer, a merciless predator without compassion or pity, but it was also one of the noblest of our wild creatures, a law unto itself and an inimitably beautiful sight in the Highland sky. But, of course, it wasn't really the eagle I was weeping for; I was a very young man still, and I could only weep for me. On the edge of manhood, and all my eagles had fallen; my wonderful father, brave and able, who I would cheerfully have died for and who would have been able to guide me through the increasingly challenging swamp land of my life; my beautiful mother, courted and won by an unprincipled gold-digger and probably a murderer, and my writing and professional future, amounting to a mediocre degree and a total absence of any gainful employment. Here was the proud Murray son and heir, sitting around weeping like a whipped boy who doesn't know what he's been whipped for.

I stopped myself and worked on replacing my shameful sobbing with a murderous determination to bring to rough justice the man I conceived responsible for it. Improvising digging tools with rocks shaped for the purpose, along with my bare hands, I buried the eagle and all of its detritus I could find, washing my hands in a nearby stream.

Two days later, in the early Saturday afternoon, I had found my strategic place. As a prominent member of the neighbouring Murrays, I was entitled to one of the best guns available, and with it stretched across my knees, I had concealed myself behind a rock at the base of one of the hills which I knew the birds would be driven over. I had moved ahead of the main group, taking advantage of the privileged freedom of movement allowed me, and I knew Uncle Stuart and his companions, including Ian Lessiter himself, were not far behind me and would soon come comfortably within range. As the birds came over the hill and flew on into the distance, I would raise myself up and shoot at them, though one or two shots would find their way into Uncle Stuart. Two, accurately placed, should do the trick. Dreadful shooting accident, who'd have thought, well, it happens, for all that, it happens, when guns are abroad. And a boy still in mourning for his recently deceased father is maybe not such a reliable shot as he might otherwise be. Such a dreadful year for the Murrays. But there again, these things happen, don't they?

I knew it would be no more than fifteen minutes at most before the man I wanted to come into view did so. I had no intention of giving way to weak, irresolute reflections, but what then happened is something I have never really been able to categorise.

Did he appear behind me, Dougal Murray in his prime, pale and shadowy like a phantom apparition? No, he didn't. Did his voice come echoing down the hill at me, calling out like some lost spirit?

No, it didn't. The apparition was all in my mind, and the voice like a disembodied whisper which communicated ideas without having to articulate them in so many precisely defined words.

Be aware. Stuart saved my life several times, as I saved his. Be aware. He loved your mother almost as much as I did, and he gave way because she chose me. Be aware. Once in a blue moon, harnesses fail; invisible deterioration, hitherto unrealised missing internal part, untraceable consequences of exposure to extreme climate conditions.

Remember. Violence and vengeance are a downward spiral, kill or be killed, until, like the mightiest and proudest eagle, your own fall will come. Remember. The eagle's blood is still on your hands, human blood is about to follow, and soon, inevitably, your blood will be on someone else's hands. Remember. Your mother's heart has been broken once; breaking it again will finish her for ever. Remember. You have almost discarded two people, your lover and your brother, who care for you deeply; you are about to break their hearts as well. Remember, Duncan, remember. These things are true, and you know them to be so.

The words, sentiments, assertions, were invisible, but they were not there in my head because of my own independent consciousness. Someone external to me put them there. I found myself looking round me, ridiculously, for someone, anyone, who was in my vicinity. But there was nothing but the air, the sky and the braying conversation of well-bred voices, growing gradually louder.

I was confused and disturbed to the point of being unable to move. I heard Uncle Stuart and his companions passing, followed by volleys of shots heading over the hill. I stayed exactly where I was, frozen to total immobility. And then I fell asleep.

I woke, with an awareness of having been somewhere without knowing where it was. It was cold and getting on for dark; there still, ridiculously, seemed to be a gun across my lap.

I made my way back to the imposing, ex-castle of the Lessiters, feeling strangely as if I'd just been released, like a penal sentence had been served. And near the front entrance, amongst all the SUVs and jeeps, was a more modest vehicle I recognised, a bright little orange Fiat which, however gloriously out of place it looked, meant more to me than all the rest of the vehicles on show put together. Josie was there in the house, and so was my brother James, both of them avowed non-shooters, but both of them expressing their anxiety for me, leading them to concoct their plan to intercept me here and find out just what was going on.

What followed was one of the great nights of my life. The beast had lifted from my back, and suddenly the person I was had reasserted himself. And half way through the evening, I found myself sitting next to Uncle Stuart, there in the enormous foyer of the place, when whoever he had been talking to left him to get another drink or something, at the same time as my conversation with my intriguing cousin soon to be stepsister Alison, now climbing partner to James, stopped when a friend came to talk to her.

We were both well mellowed with good food and drink, and I found myself looking him straight in the eyes, relaxed, even friendly, now. Dare I, I thought, and discovered I did.

'Tell me, Uncle Stuart, were you and my father ever in competition over my mother?'

He looked at me at first with a 'what kind of a question is that?' expression on his face, but something in my tone, and perhaps the use of the uncle again, seemed to reassure him.

'Let's take a little night air, Duncan', he said. Outside, on a bench in the gardens and free from the noise and heat, I heard every distinct word.

'Yes, we were. I was in the same hotel, and I fell in love with her at the same time'.

'And you did what – withdraw in his favour?'

'No, not really. I would like to be able to say so, but there wasn't that kind of nobility to it. I loved your father dearly, Duncan, but we were in competition in almost every respect from toddlers onwards, until we realised co-operation worked better. And in any case, your mother would not allow herself to be some puppet for us to fight over. She made her own choice, and she chose your father'.

He looked at me with a sudden curious intensity.

'And, of course, if you want to know the truth, every time I ever look at you, I am reminded of his victory. You are both him and her, mentally and physically, the very epitome of their relationship. If I haven't been as affectionate an uncle to you as I should have been, Duncan, that is some kind of explanation, but an inadequate one. I know I can never replace your father, nor will I try, but perhaps I can make up a little for not being much of an uncle'.

We shook hands and managed a kind of clumsy embrace, and as I turned from it, I saw my mother standing at a window watching us, and there was an expression on her face which I hadn't seen since my father died, a serenity and satisfaction that somehow signified a kind of closure for me. It seemed like the fall of my last eagle, perhaps the wildest and most vicious of them all, a wild beast hovering not for food but for vengeance. Poisoned by imagined grievance, it looks for some innocent lamb to vent its spleen upon. Only my father's gentle but authoritative voice – because I shall remain convinced, to my dying day, that's essentially what it was – was capable of downing that last eagle. In my mind, I buried it and all that accompanied it, like the golden eagle, in the ground of Scotland.

Writing this has been cathartic for me. My mother, never as scrupulous about checking her health as she should have been, was diagnosed with a cancer too late to stop it, and died in 2004, only in her late sixties. Stuart, as I called him until the day he died, was devastated and never the same again; he died in his bed eight years later of a sudden heart attack.

So now, my good lady Josie and I, assisted by our full and growing family, rule the Murray estate, stewards of the land rather than rulers over it. The Murray eagles fly again, and that voice, whatever or whoever it was, is still there for me as and when either of us judges that it needs to be.

PICTURES OF PAULA

My sister Paula is holding open the front door of our grandparents' house. She is eleven, I am eight. She is quick, whippet thin, and always moving; her eyes, her mouth, her stick legs poking out of a hated flowery skirt. I love and fear her at the same time; she can and has both made my days and destroyed them. But we have never had a day like this before, and I have never relied on her as much as this before.

Now, she is frozen. Even the pale grey eyes which unsettle people have a film of fear over them. Those eyes can mock me; she knows more than I do, and fears less. Suddenly, she is a statue of terror.

I look to her left and the police car is there in huge proximity, blue and white with an orange beacon on top, and my mind can only deal with boy questions about whether we will hear its siren der – der –der – der – and whether they will let me look over the gleaming dashboard.

Grandma and Grandad are being helped from the back seat by policemen, and Grandma has her hankie over her face, as she does when she thinks her God isn't being as good to her as He ought to be. God has just taken her son and daughter-in-law away from her, and she cannot, for the moment at least, cope with God.

I look back at Paula. Her eyes widen and her hand twitches quickly on the door frame.

She weeps alarmingly quickly, as if there were pipes in the back of her eyes, and the sight intrigues me so much I forget to weep myself.

'Oh, Davey', she says, her voice faded to shadow. 'What's to happen now?'

As we watch the approaching procession, her bony arm has encircled me like a long friendly snake and I can smell the morning soap on her cheek.

I'm eleven and she's fourteen. I wake and blink the sleep and sweat out of my eyes to see her looking down on me. I have woken too quickly for her to arrange her disguise, and her face is a naked mask of anxiety, the eyes gleaming. I urgently want to do or say something to reassure her, even though she is so fond of goading and mocking me. I am almost naked, with only a small pair of pants on. But I don't care, and neither does she; none of that stuff has ever bothered us, however much it might bother the Grans. My throat is so sore I can't speak, my head aches intensely, and I am awash with trickling sweat.

Grandma came in and ordered me to get myself into pyjamas, then she went out again. I obeyed her with some difficulty, then she returned, shut all the windows, pulled the big curtains and switched on the electric fire. I threw off the pyjama jacket almost immediately and the trousers not long after that. The pants would have gone too, but complete nakedness could offend the Grans, especially Grandma, and I am still young enough not to want to do that; they are all I have left of Mum and Dad. As I dozed, I must have kicked off the bedclothes as well.

I look up again; her eyes rake me up and down, the eyebrows almost joined in the middle, as if looking for answers, or at least a way of identifying the right questions. Then she explodes abruptly into action – bang, bang, bang, the way she does. She opens two windows, pulls a curtain back and turns the fire off. She pulls the eiderdown and blankets right off the bed.

Grandma is alerted by the swish of the curtains; she comes in and screeches.

'Heavens above, cover him! He'll catch his death!' she says, and picks up a blanket.

The following confrontation has been coming for a while, though I am genuinely surprised to be the cause of it.

'Leave it'. Paula is standing facing her; she's as big now, and her tone is crisp, commanding. 'Leave it, Grandma'.

Grandma flutters, hands twisting on the edge of a blanket, half up and half down.

'He's almost naked, child; he'll get cold, and it's not decent'.

'He's too hot; he's in his own bed in his own room. He's entitled to be as naked as the day he was born if he chooses. Leave it'.

We have lived with the Grans ever since the remains of my mother and father were scooped up off that motorway. We pray in church, before food, before bed, for Grandma's son, my father, and his 'chosen woman'. Grandma cannot bring herself to utter her name, apparently because she had been married before she married my father. When we pray, Paula kneels with her hands over her face, supposedly praying but actually doing an accurate mickey-take of Grandma's intricate hand wringing with her handkerchief. She looks at me and makes me laugh with kissing movements of her mouth. I laugh, Paula laughs, Grandma gets cross, and the crosser she gets, the more difficult Paula finds it to stop smirking. Grandad is always in some other world, looking but not seeing, as he has been ever since my father died. But recently, Paula doesn't find Grandma funny any more; Grandma has moved beyond her defiance to her scorn. Just before sleep envelops me again, I hear the door closing and I know very well who's leaving the room.

When I wake up, I have a blanket covering my lower half and

a glass and jug of water next to the bed. I am much cooler, the fever is ebbing away, the head and throat have eased, and I doze off again, much more peacefully, yes, but still with the image of my sister toe to toe with Grandma, the grey eyes blazing.

'Leave it'.

I am fourteen, she is seventeen. I'm late home from school. No genius at much of the schoolwork, I have gratefully discovered that I can run, steadily and for miles, and be valued for it. My coach Mr. Tyler is a respected athlete who runs for the region and the local athletics club, and he is giving me, in his taciturn but tolerant way, a place to belong. When he orders his protégés, now amazingly including me, to stay behind and train, we stay behind and train. I need someone I can respect enough to obey. I don't think Paula does, or if she does, she has yet to find the person.

She left school last year and the rumours about what she is doing and who she is seeing have hovered over her ever since. She comes and goes as she pleases, and the Grans are too frightened of her to say anything.

I take the short cut through the park; Tyler's training is thorough, and my legs are aching. Through the trees ahead of me, I see Paula's back about seventy yards away. I know Paula's back well enough, and in any case, she has her garish blue top on, the one with silvery threads through it, probably visible from half a mile away. Only Paula wears a party top at five thirty in the afternoon. I don't know why, and it worries me that I don't know why.

I think of shouting something at her, brother/sister banter, because these days I give as good as I get. We have declared UDI with the Grans, and like the fun of sparring with each other. We are the same height now, so she can't look down at me with her withering eyes and nose in the air.

My mouth is actually opening to shout when I see a car glide suddenly in front of her. She hurries across, as if relieved. Her head is leaning right down into the open window; I hear stereo laughter, her light, wheedling voice against a male baritone. I move into the trees on my right and get close enough to see her face lit up artificially, as if she's playing a part for all it's worth. When she laughs, her head goes right back and her right foot describes little uncertain circles on the ground.

As she gets into the back of the car, I look down at the grass and muck; there is a used syringe in the dead leaves to my right, and a discarded blob at the foot of a tree trunk. I look up to see her face turned directly towards me. I move behind a tree. My eyes are wet, my face is burning and I struggle to catch my breath.

Just over a year later, on a Thursday afternoon, I come home early to pack my kit up for an evening athletics meeting. There is a large estate car parked outside the house. Grandma always does her shopping on Thursdays, unenthusiastically accompanied by Grandad, and the Grans don't have a car. I duck behind a car on the other side of the road to watch.

Two men emerge, both of them well over six feet tall, heavily built with tattooed arms and sullen, disinterested faces. They are carrying large boxes. And following them, with a smaller box of her own, is Paula.

She is trying to organise them as they bump down the boxes in the back of the estate car. They carry on regardless of her; they fetch a few more boxes from the house, and all the time they mostly ignore her and joke between themselves as Paula flits about distractedly, alternately trying to order them and mollify them.

When the men are in sitting in the front seat, one of them shouts towards the house and swears; I can just about hear his words, and even as a teenage boy used to bad language around me, I blush briefly; the other man chuckles. Paula hurries out and gets in the back, pretending to be angry with him. I stand up and look across the street, to see and keep another picture, this time an anguished, conflicted face turned unseeingly in my direction, the grey eyes ringed below and the mouth forming words which I cannot decipher.

The car speeds away and her face seems to appear again at the back window, but within seconds, the car has disappeared.

'She only took what was hers', was all Gran had to say via the twisted handkerchief, though I think she is secretly relieved.

I am twenty, and in a taxi with three friends, on the stag night of a twenty-two year old quiet man called Mark who is on the fringe of international recognition. For Tyler's runners during the season, too much drink is likely to bring Tyler 'down on your head, son, like a ton of bricks', so this has to be a modest do; we have been into the centre of Nottingham, our nearest city, for a few civilised drinks and now we are taxiing back to the hotel where the wedding will take place tomorrow.

We pass behind the bus station and the traffic slows, partly because of the endless sequence of traffic lights, but also because cars are pulling to the side to talk to girls who emerge from the shadows into arcs of light from the street lamps. Mark seems to leer over at a girl as the light falls on her and then he grins at me across the back seat.

'You can forget all that stuff, buddy', I say. 'You're spoken for, as of tomorrow'.

He nods sagely and grins again; he's happy enough, and I'm not surprised – I know the girl he's marrying. I thought I might have had a chance myself, but **the** girl hasn't happened for me yet. Girls have; **the** girl hasn't. As I watch one young woman move determinedly towards a car, another immediately steps into the light.

Her hair is pinned up, and her shoes so high-heeled that she looks four inches taller, but it is certainly Paula. I haven't seen her for a while, but I can still identify her just by the shape, just by the angle of the head. The taxi slows again and for a horrific moment

I am paralysed with dread that she will walk across to us, but the driver spots a gap, and we whisk quickly on past. My gorge rises and I only just manage to control the beer inside me. As I regain control, my hands are sweating, and I know well enough that Paula in the streetlight is a picture which will remain with me for ever.

I am twenty two. I work at the sports centre and live in a flat share, while concentrating on running and getting my coaching badges. Mary, one of the centre receptionists, is the girl I've been seeing and we both think it will soon be serious enough for us to live together. It is already serious in the lovemaking sense, and I am still adjusting to the new reality that **the** girl might really have happened for me.

As I pack my kit away, the Centre manager, an amiable and competent guy called Mike Richards, comes into the changing room.

'Pop into the office on your way out, David, lad, will you?' he says.

In the office, he hands me a purple, slightly scented envelope.

'A woman insisted that I handed this to you personally, and then left'.

'Who was she?'

'I don't know. But if I was to describe her, David, and I'm not being funny, honestly, she looked like you in drag. And amazingly, quite pretty, for all that'.

Only in the privacy of my own room did I eventually allow myself to open the letter.

Dear David,

You're not going to believe it, Davey, but I've scored properly at last. A decent man, instead of the chancers and losers who usually stick to me as if I'm a magnet. He's a Canadian guy I met in a club. I was doing bar work, and a bit of cooking. Anything but the game. I'll not deny it, Davey; I saw you see me once, and I nearly died. Anyway, enough of walking the wild side. More than enough. I'm going off back across the Atlantic to marry him; his name's Doug, and he's a teacher, would you believe. I should have kept in touch, I know, but I didn't want to involve you and the Grans, while the pimps still had hold of me. But I lost them off eventually; a good police guy actually stuck his oar in for me. Think of me, David. Maybe, if it all works out, we'll see each other again. I've heard you're courting, and she looks really nice. I wish you everything you want for yourself and more, Davey. Perhaps you'll understand and forgive one day.

Love, Paula.

I am thirty four, and taking it easy with my paper after a long day. I'm the manager of the leisure centre now. I married Mary and inherited when Grandma died three years after Grandad; she left everything to me, and it was much more than I expected.

My kids Matthew and Paula are upstairs talking to their friends on their phones, crazy as it is, since most of them only live a few streets away.

Matt calls down the stairs. I thought the peace too good to last.

'Dad, there's this crazy lady on the screen from Canada who wants to talk to you. Keeps saying is Davey there. Davey?' He giggles and I hear his sister giggling too. I take the stairs two at a time. The kids see my face; their eyebrows shoot up and their smiles disappear.

'The picture keeps fuzzing off and on. Storms in the Atlantic or something', Matt says, and at first, all I can see is a blurred outline of what is probably a head. Then it clears, and there she is, a little fuller in the chin, with short, neat hair and those grey eyes, once again intense and with the laughter back in them, enough to silence both the kids into just sitting and staring.

'Hello, David', she says. 'I'm just getting to know my niece and nephew'.

Yes, Mary and I should have told them by now and haven't, maybe because we couldn't decide what or how to tell them or whether we would be starting something which might never be resolved, except badly. We decided we could at least name our daughter after her. They are looking across at me now with mouths and eyes as wide as they'll go, and their studied kiddie cool has flown out of the window. It is such a moment that I can't stop tears starting into my eyes, and I don't remember the last time that happened. This freaks the kids even more; they are suddenly frozen solid, looking at each other for reassurance.

'Hello, Paula', I say, as I nod to the kids and smile. 'Give me a minute with the kids and then we'll talk'.

It's time to give my kids the reassurance they need from the only person who can supply it.

'I'm going to explain all this to you soon, and make my excuses about why we didn't explain it to you before. But yes, this lady is your aunt. Say hello to your Aunt Paula'. And they do; a little automaton-like, a little strained, but they do. She hears them.

And then perhaps the most memorable picture of all, the grey eyes at peace.

MAKING THE GRADES

Jennifer sits straight-backed and still, watching me dispassionately through blue-green eyes. She is a model of self-possession, her uniform as neat as her trimmed short black hair. I ask her my first set question.

'Do you have a system for revision?'

'Oh, yes. I use colour-coded compartments, with different colours for each subject and a check-list of topics covered. Sad, really. Almost obsessional'.

'Do people say that about it?'

A quick, dismissive smile and sideways nod of the head.

'It's not much talked about. You're expected to sort it out for yourself'.

Later, the distraction question arrives; I am already trying not to make it sound formulaic.

'You're not obliged to tell me anything, but is there anything happening in the background which interferes with your exam work or distracts you from it?'

A heavy pause; her eyes cloud and she shuffles restlessly. The words emerge hesitantly.

'My father can be very ... bad-tempered. He is ill, sometimes. We do what we can'.

I see again that border between research and intrusion. 'Bad tempered' echoes a question mark in the air.

Mick leans forward, his arms resting loosely on the chair arms and his hands occasionally moving. His light hair is tousled and unkempt, his tie dragged down. He smiles, frequently but fleetingly, almost in self-parody.

'I haven't got a clue what I'm doing, really', he says. 'I look at books now and then. Sometimes it goes in, sometimes it doesn't. I don't worry about it'.

Later, I ask him the 'distractions' question. He grimaces and looks out of the window.

'It's difficult with the team sometimes. I play weekends, sometimes week nights. I can't always make it'. He gives me an odd sideways assessing look.

'Why – because you're revising?'

'Because I'm trying to'.

His eyes stray to the window again; his right hand twitches across his leg.

'I'm trying to', he says again.

My brief was to find out how A level students handled exam courses – planning and revision programmes, the help available, and the obstacles, academic and otherwise. Questionnaires provided the statistics and interviews the personal details. February, two months before the exams, was becoming pressurised, and yet it seemed that one in five students were doing part-time jobs for at least twelve hours a week, and one in ten had 'carer' responsibilities for relatives. The schools generally left revision to the students, whose approach ranged from the hyper-organised Jennifer to the clueless Mick.

My main 'distraction' at the time was my father's situation. After my mother's death four years previously, Dad had 'downsized' into a bungalow. As usual, he saw it as simple practicality; 'I cannot take care of a large house or afford to pay someone else to. It's perfectly simple, Peter'. A favourite phrase. For me, the house remained full of Mum; he clearly missed her like hell, and it worried me that he didn't want to acknowledge it or talk about it. He was also ill; there had been at least one serious angina 'incident' which the hospital had eventually decreed was not a heart attack. He had supposedly given up smoking, but I constantly felt I could detect it in his bungalow.

He was clearly dubious about my leaving teaching for research. I wasn't paid as much as I had been in teaching, and he thought, even if he didn't articulate it, that I was imposing an unreasonable burden on Helen, my wife, who he considered himself to be championing.

'Dad, Helen helped with my application. The whole thing was partly her idea'.

'Well, you have always been good at adapting people to your way of thinking, Peter'.

Our meetings often included truce-like silences like the one which followed this remark, as if we were both retreating to our corners to consult our trainers. Mum had always occupied the space between us, and now it gaped very emptily at times.

Sarah has brought a notebook in with her. As we talk, this and her pen become the main outlets for a fidgety disposition. She is small and quick; her eyes visit me and depart again every few seconds.

'I visit Nan a lot', she says. 'Take work there sometimes'.

'Your grandmother?'

'Yes. She's not well'.

'Oh. I'm sorry'.

'I stay over there sometimes. Her place is quieter than ours. Tommy and Liza banging about; I can't concentrate'.

'Do you get as much done as you want to?'

'Well, I don't know'. The notebook is abandoned at last.
'How do you know when enough is enough?'

Matthew is broad-shouldered and heftily built, with black-rimmed spectacles, dark eyes and a rather supercilious manner.

'Most of them', he says of his fellow students, 'are hopeless, especially the boys. Most of them pretend they're not bothered, but secretly, they're terrified. Only the top grades are any use now, and only a few stand a chance. I'm going to enjoy', he says, bumping up in his chair, 'being top of the class, when the results come out'.

He reads a question in my face.

'They think people who work hard should be ashamed of it. They make snide remarks and behave childishly –'

He abruptly changes direction.

'Anyway, you wanted to know something about my methods –'

'Yes, please'.

'I have a wall chart with the three subjects and all the topics within each. I cross off squares when they've been revised. The teachers haven't covered the full syllabus yet, and I don't want sudden late surprises. It makes sense to me'.

'It makes sense to me, too. Can you work in peace at home?'

He shrinks back a little.

'Oh, yes. They even keep the television turned down. Oh, no problem there'.

As February moved into March, the students' mounting tension was communicating itself to me, or so it seemed to Helen.

'You spend longer in the study. And you're developing monosyllabic tendencies'.

I'd remarked about student angst rubbing off on me. I glanced at her in surprise.

'It's to be expected, Peter', Helen said. 'It would surprise me if you didn't empathise. Professional neutrality, yes, but they're all young and vulnerable. And then, of course, there's your father. Perhaps you're seeing your younger self. Perhaps your Dad and the kids have you pointing in two directions at once.'

I couldn't deny that the seventeen year old Peter Holdsworth had occasionally reappeared in my life, as my interviewing caught the students' insecurities and fears of failure. My father, at that time, was a university History lecturer, fond of telling me how mistakes repeat themselves. A professorial chair eluded him until his gathering heart problems forced retirement. As the only child, I saw him on a ladder, beckoning me to pass him and climb to heights beyond what he had achieved. And I resisted. Even at seventeen, I knew that we were different people; like my mother, I had more worldliness and less of the academic ambition that characterised my father.

The inevitable confrontation happened in early March, as the students plunged gallantly on or began to struggle. I visited my father and found him complaining of chest pains. A faint aroma of tobacco hung in the air, and a button of anger within me was pushed.

'You are obviously smoking, Dad, in spite of your specific undertakings to me and Mum'.

He gave me the familiar long, weary look, and his face turned so far from me that I could only just make out his words.

'How extraordinary, the two of you conspiring against me beyond the grave'.

I was suddenly on my feet, and his upturned eyes were genuinely alarmed.

'If she'd looked after her own health as assiduously as she tried to look after yours, she might just have found out what was wrong with her in time. Your indifference to your well-being is one thing; your indifference to hers was quite another'.

Tears appeared in his eyes.

'I urged her to go for check-ups. At surgery reception, she

considered that she saw endless hypochondriacs and inadequates and hated the possibility of becoming one of them. What did I ever do to you, Peter, to explain this innate hostility of yours? I have never been cruel; I have always tried to encourage and support. If I was ever harsh, it was because I wanted you to succeed, for your sake. Don't make your failure my fault, Peter. I did my best. As I did with your mother'.

And, with that, he retreated to his room. Once again, he had defined the bizarre way he saw things and left me to like it or lump it. And, at last, he had declared that he perceived me as having 'failed', and characterised my mother's illness as, ultimately, her own fault. As usual, everything was everyone else's fault, and George Holdsworth battled heroically on to make them realise their own shortcomings.

A boy with the elastic build and confident manner of young sportsmen, Richard is jacketless in a bright white shirt and neat tie. His long legs stretch out, his hands rest on his thighs.

'I suppose it's being shut indoors which makes the revision difficult', he says.

'Do you need high grades? You mentioned sponsorship'.

'Yes, the sponsorship looks on. My aunt thinks so, and she's been very helpful; she is a professional herself, a tennis coach'.

'I suppose good grades would be a kind of insurance, wouldn't they?'

'You sound like my mother'. His grin is conspiratorial and infectious. He carries on.

'My aunt and my parents don't see eye to eye. I have to referee occasionally. But my aunt is living it, if you like, being a pro. My gut instinct is with her'.

He leans back in his seat.

'I'll try to get the indoor slog out of the way first. Then I'll give the tennis a go. It will needs hard work, but it's for something, isn't it? Money, for a start'.

I nod emphatically, without quite understanding why.

Katherine's long, groomed hair frames her face, and the blue eyes are alive and concentrated. Her cheeks, though, have a hint of gauntness, and her calves are unexpectedly thin.

'Everything else has just had to take a back seat. Even Stuart'.

'Your boyfriend?'

'Yes. Very protective; jealous, really, at times. But career has to come first, especially now'.

'Career?'

'Modelling. My mother found this brilliant agency. Quite expensive – Dad moans, of course – but with girls who are really going places. The A levels matter, all the same; models can't afford to be brainless bimbos these days'.

This statement has a recycled sound to it.

'So you don't find revision too much of a struggle?'

'Just one more discipline, really. Weight, exercise, diet, revision. They all need to be planned and programmed'.

'Will you have a contract, do you think, by the time you leave school?'

'Well, the agency thinks so; they're doing their best. My mother thinks so. Dad is not so optimistic. But, then, it's not really a guy thing, is it?'

A steady, pleading look in the blue eyes and, once again, I am nodding vigorously.

After a few days, my father and I manage a kind of reconciliation by phone. Faults on both sides – pressure of work, me, missing my mother, him.

'Ignore that nonsense about failure, Peter, please. I am so stricken with frustration at times that I will tear at people with anything, logical or otherwise. You are clearly on the way to a

Master's degree; talk of failure is absurd'.

'Neither did I mean to make it sound as if I thought you'd neglected Mum. I have to watch my words very carefully these days, and the dam bursts occasionally. And, of course, it didn't come out right. Does that make any sense?'

So we concreted over our weeds again, and waited for them to peep back up through the slabs. I pleaded pressure of work, not without some justification; I had set myself an ambitious interview programme and had a mountain of statistical evidence to unpack. However, by the end of March, I felt that if I didn't see my father soon, the relationship might disappear into a void of neglect, and I hurried round after a session at the school nearest to his house after agreeing the visit with him the day before.

Immediately after letting myself in, I knew the character of the silence was wrong. I found him lying full length between the living room and conservatory, on his side, almost embryonic; his breathing was hardly audible. I called 999 and waited, terrified at the pallor of his face and appalled at my utter powerlessness.

They were there in just over ten minutes, and what followed was a timeless period with everyone locked into semi-automatic procedures and routines. After a short panic in the ambulance when Dad appeared to become comatose, they reassured me that he was only sleeping. He drifted in and out of sleep, but even when awake, he didn't know where he was or what was happening.

As Dad was taken to the intensive care ward, I tried to stifle the panic reverberating around me and the ominous suspicions of Dad's smoking. I found that again, even when my father should have been the only person on my mind, my thoughts kept returning to my young interviewees. I knew, from both interview and statistical material, that the kind of situation I had with my father was not untypical for them during the examination year – relatives, friends or even they themselves could and did face health or even bereavement problems. Not for the first time in my experience of research, some of the most pertinent questions simply couldn't be asked. If a thirty-six year old man finds himself floundering in this situation, how could people who were much younger and less experienced in meeting these crises deal with them? I knew many people would always argue that, if the year on year results are getting better, there is no case for anxiety about exam stress, as if the price being paid for such success is a matter of no account. As if having lots of people with good grades is more important than the possibility that a proportion of them might be heading towards mental illness and possible addiction problems. As if thousands of identical grades allow each any real significance.

I moved myself forcibly away from the research issues and concentrated on my father's crisis. Eventually, we were able to talk. He was linked to a large green monitor above the bed. He was pale and exhausted; I expected him to also be frightened, but he didn't seem to be. There was a kind of fatalism in his tone which didn't ease my anxiety. We held hands, something we hadn't done since I was a child.

'Pushing my luck, Peter', he said, with a grimace of a smile. 'Thank God you were there. I'm so sorry to have caused you such alarm'.

The words amounted to the civilised standards, the proper behaviour, he always observed, but something struck me as unconvincing about it. In my gut, in that depth where we keep our awareness of the unpalatable but undeniable, I knew the only person in the world really capable of keeping his essential will to live afloat had gone, permanently and irretrievably.

March moved into April; the exams were now very imminent indeed. The juxtaposition of the research and my father's situation caused me further soul-searching. Had Dad taken my research detachment and thrown it out of the window? Most students didn't seem to have too much difficulty; was I underestimating the strength and durability of the young?

I concluded, in the temporising way of researchers, that it was too early to know. Both personal and professional situations were still to be resolved. Some schools were becoming uncertain about interviews continuing; I had to judge whether or not I had enough material, and whether interviewing them at the very edge of the season justified taking revision time from them. For the moment, the schools accepted my arguments about the need for evidence from this stage, and students were still willing to volunteer.

My father stayed in hospital for the best part of two weeks, and the incident was clearly understood to have been a heart attack. The doctors suspected neglected medication and smoking. I knew I could go to the bungalow and strip it of all smoking materials, but my father was a resourceful man and that wouldn't hinder him for long if he was determined about it. And I couldn't help but hark back to a few occasions when I had considered myself an adult when he obviously didn't. Decisions had been taken which I'd regarded at the time as high-handed, and acting in a similar fashion when the boot was on the other foot would strike me as hypocrisy. Even if my father was making wrong choices, I couldn't justify taking away his right to make them. To do so from a sense of duty would be presumptuous – duty to whom? – and to do so as some kind of 'payback' would be deeply distasteful.

The relationship between parent and child is evolutionary, and many of the 'thens' which had formed my relationship with Dad were, I knew, the 'nows' for my students, being moulded for better or worse by pressurised exam times. I wondered whether the source of Jennifer's father's 'bad temper' – drink, depression – would colour her feelings for him for ever afterwards; whether Sarah, staying with her grandmother away from the clatter of her siblings, would drift inexorably away from her own home; whether the battle between Richard's parents and his aunt would eventually exclude one or the other; whether Katherine's suspicious father might prove right, and at what cost, against her optimistic mother, and whether anyone could intervene to help poor adrift Mick. When their choices had to be made with or by their parents, which memories would resound the most?

Deborah is large rather than fat, and exudes a generosity of spirit in her booming voice and air of general bonhomie. She is smiling good-naturedly as I thank her for talking to me at this prime revision time.

'Well, I don't seem to need it too much, to tell you the truth', she says, and it sounds more apologetic than arrogant. 'I generally find that stuff stays with me. I never have done much revision, and I'm doing alright so far'.

These April interviewees typically included more students at the extremes of super confident and fatalistically resigned.

'It's quite a gift'.

'Oh, yes, I know. I usually keep quiet; it sounds vaguely like gloating'.

'Do you think it will continue through university? You've got an offer lined up, I take it?'

'Oh, yes. The sooner the better. Get the hell out of here, pardon my French'.

'You don't like the school?'

'Not so much the school. Well, between you and me, Mum and Dad, bless them, are getting on a bit – I was something of a fertility last chance saloon, basically – and they're lovely, but a bit slow, and they will keep saying appalling things about race and gays. I mean, I would come out, but I just don't dare. Uni will be easier'.

Escape, from a variety of personal circumstances, is one prime A level motivation which has never been given quite the emphasis that it should.

Des is small for his age, and looks more fifteen than seventeen. He is one more case of the cruelty of adolescent development that I've seen in the chair facing me. He sits leaning forward, and in between his words, his gaze returns to the floor. There is something fearful, withdrawn, in his eyes.

'Dad makes me go up and get on with it', he says. 'Or else'.

Yet again, a signpost in the direction of a dead end.

'You have to work or be punished?'

The silence is suddenly electric.

'Yes. Well, you know, Dad wants me to do better than – than him, I suppose. 'You'll thank me for it, Desmond, one day,' he says, before he starts'.

Starts? Starts what? Research/intrusion boundary arrived at again.

'I spend a lot of time pretending I'm doing it, but I don't really understand most of it. When the results come out, Dad's going to…do his nut…'

The eyes go down and stay down.

The results were covered in the educational press, highlighting the gender differences – girls used a much larger variety of methods, and started earlier – and the huge figures for part-time work and caring responsibilities. The report also made clear that the assumption on the part of many teachers, that students would find their own ways to revise, was inaccurate in the case of a significant proportion of the A level population. Each school got a copy of their own results, and remained anonymous in the media material.

Jennifer had a high offer of two As and a B for her first choice university, but her colour-coding obviously worked, because she got them, whatever her father's 'bad temper' might have been about.

Mick's more modest target of two Bs and a C proved to be too much. He got two Cs, and failed to turn up for one exam altogether. His tutor's understanding was that Mick himself had elected to work with his uncle, a plumber, and qualify himself in that line. I suspect Mick had had as much 'academe' as he could stomach.

Sarah applied to do a nursing degree, and she did meet the grade requirements, thereby starting on a career for which she had already carefully prepared.

Matthew got all of the three As he needed and a place in a prestigious university. One of his teachers said that he'd seemed genuinely happy to be leaving. It's only to be hoped that the enormous effort he made towards those grades left him enough to survive in the highly competitive environment of his university.

Richard got indifferent A levels, two Bs and a C, but one university accepted him largely on the basis of his sporting ability and he undertook a course to qualify as a P.E. teacher and tennis coach, suggesting a parental victory on points.

Katharine's results were also mediocre, two Cs and a B. She hadn't applied to a university, being intent on a modelling career, but in late August a teacher who'd known her told me that the agency in which her mother had invested was no longer in business.

Deborah got her excellent results, three As, and her escape. A teacher said that she had appeared briefly at the school on results day and had already made arrangements to stay with a student she knew at the university, an ex-sixth former of the school.

Desmond's direction was difficult to establish. His A levels were disastrous; one entry withdrawn, and a D and an unclassified for the other two. His tutor later understood that he had left home for a flat share and some details of his 'case' were sub judice.

My father lived for another ten years. He engaged fully with the rehabilitation classes following his release from hospital, and formed a relationship which he told me was entirely platonic, as if that was any business of mine, with a widowed neighbour. He was 79, and although it was a heart attack which killed him, I never did see or smell any evidence of a smoking habit after he came out of hospital following the first attack.

My own son arrived not long after this research, and is now in his teens. I have scrupulously set myself to be a good father, but I cannot deny that he does test my patience and my understanding at times. I may or may not make the grade, but I am doing my best.

THE BARD OF BROOKVALE

I won't go into detail about what Jay and I had done just before she cajoled me into our 'project'. This isn't that kind of story. Enough to say that it was one of those special moments for relaxing and contemplating the joys of love.

> *At the end of the day, there's me and there's Jay*
> *scampering under blankets like kids in a den;*
> *at the end of every game, the joke is the same,*
> *the giggles to be had between women and men.*
> Rob Fuller, aged 20, on campus

'You will need to go home to your parents for a few weeks, Rob', she seemed to be saying to my still cloud-floating mind. 'It can't be so terrible, can it? You lived there for a long time before you came to uni'.

'Jay', I said, 'what exactly are you talking about?'

She raked me with her eyes, but not necessarily for the right reasons. She could switch from amorous to everyday in seconds, and it could be disconcerting at times.

'We need a flat, Rob. Campus is too much hassle. Wendy Watmore's in that block next door, and I swear she presses glasses against the wall. And I don't know what would've happened if Ellen or Megan had wandered in'.

I looked at her, not for the first time, in open-mouthed amazement.

'Don't you lock the door?'

'Oh, not much. You just never know. When I was with Danny, he pulled his what's it – hamstring? – at a crucial moment and Ellen had to help even while he was still -'

She saw my face.

'Well, never mind. He was just a fling, Rob, before I started with you –'

'As in last term. Anyway, this flat; do you really want to share it with me, or is it just about getting away from Ellen and Megan?'

She did something unmentionable, and then snuggled up to me.

'You just sweet talk your obliging folks into helping us with a deposit – even renting now, you have to put something down – and I will do the same, so we can have a place of our own. Just think what we could do in a place of our own'.

I was thinking, which soon became obvious, and so, it seems, was she. Interlude.

Only after that did I realise what I'd let myself in for, re. my 'obliging folks'. Though I'd been with Jay for nearly four weeks, I still hadn't got round to telling her the full story of who and what my folks amounted to.

> *Brookvale Gardens is an executive sentence*
> *of detached brick villas, all looking the same;*
> *Brookvale Gardens is residential nonsense*
> *as void and trivial as its P.R. name.*
> Rob Fuller, aged 17, in his Brookvale bedroom.

I found, surprisingly after the afternoon we'd shared, that I could still walk. So we strolled out to a quiet part of the campus, and sat down for a chat. Yes, we did talk to each other, Jay and me, and because I knew that my relationship with her wasn't just about sex, I decided to tell her the story. And she listened, which she did, Jay, when it mattered.

The house in Brookvale Gardens is where my family finished up about a year after my mother and father separated. I was fourteen and my sister Jo was sixteen. I was, to be honest, cut loose, adrift. It hadn't been much of a surprise when my parents split. My father, who I did try to think of as 'Dad', not always successfully, wasn't violent or drunk or any of the obvious things which split marriages; he was a neat, precise sort of man, an English teacher, who saw life in a dispassionate, academic kind of way. Mum, on the other hand, was much like me, bouncing off visible obstacles, full of enthusiams, disgusts, triumphs and defeats. She was a teacher, too, specialising in Drama; they met working on a local drama group production. What made her choose my father, I don't know; perhaps she thought his steadiness might steady her. As it was, it stifled her, and she frequently exasperated him. Being with them when Jo was somewhere else, as she was most of the time, could be trying.

> *She clattered her muesli round the bowl.*
> *He knived through his bacon with deliberation*
> *and I sat quite still, mute and little,*
> *caught in the silence like a sacrifice.*
> Rob Fuller, aged 19, remembering Rob Fuller,
> aged 13, at breakfast with Mr. and Mrs. Fuller.

So Father wafted off, without me or my sister, more surprisingly in her case than mine, because she's very like him, matter of fact, unsurprised. Being naturally self-contained, I don't think she needed him any more than he needed her.

What I wanted most, perhaps to deal with my confusion, was privacy. I put a bolt on my door and spent a lot of time in my room, feeding my mounting Brookvale paranoia.

> *I can only be me when I'm locked in a cell*
> *away from their constant asking and prying;*
> *I'm a voluntary prisoner, a solitary confiner,*
> *a boy desert island in an ocean of people.*
> Robert Fuller, aged 16 and a half, at
> Brookvale Gardens, self-locked in his room.

The man who succeeded my father in my mother's affections was a guy called Tony Peters. My mother wanted me to call him 'New Dad', as if you could buy yourself another dad when your old one ran out, like a car. Tony was everything my father wasn't – aggressively successful, man of the world, full of treats and deals. He took us into Brookvale Gardens, including Jo, to my surprise, because I had thought she couldn't stand the guy. I asked Jo why she hadn't chosen to live with my father.

'Right, Rob. It's like this; if there were no-one but you and him, would you live with him?'

I had to admit, probably not. He needed everything done exactly to his routine; his taste for routine sometimes infuriated my mother. And, even as I squirmed at the manufactured landscape and the lack of imagination of Brookvale Gardens, what Tony did for my mother soon became obvious. He took her to decent restaurants; my father could sometimes be persuaded to eat out, but to pretty basic pizza joints and the like. Tony would also put on a decent jacket to go out; my father would usually still be in his work clothes.

And as for our own house, 12 Rowan Avenue, Brookvale Gardens, modernistic and soulless it might be, but the central heating worked, the windows shut properly, the guttering didn't need constant attention, and you couldn't hear the neighbours through the walls. Pre-Brookvale Gardens, we lived in a big rambling terraced place – 'genuine period property', my father called it – which was in some ways magic for kids, with its semi-wild garden, inexplicable outhouses, a few trees big enough for climbing, but in terms of the more refined creature comforts, not too good. And for my mother, who everyone seemed to assume should do the catering, washing etc., even though she worked herself, the inadequate cooking range, the unreliable fridge, the beat up old washing machine, could between them reduce her days to drudgery. Even at 12, the imbalance registered with me.

> *Father has the paper spread across his knees,*
> *Mum's in the kitchen, boiling and sweating,*
> *Jo's in her bedroom, taking her ease,*
> *Mum's washing dishes, toiling and fretting.*
> Rob Fuller, aged 12, Inkerman Road.

Jay listened to all this as we held hands in the shadow of a big, gnarled tree near the uni perimeter fence. It was one of those still, scented evenings.

'Tony will probably put up the money for me – it would mean getting me out of his hair, maybe permanently. But I'm not sure I want to leave my mother there with him. I mean, he makes his money advising people on managing **their** money, and he seems to do alright on it, but even though I lived there for four years before leaving for uni, I never really got to know him. My father more or less abandoned Mum – or she him, I've never been certain. Tony seems to look after her, but is he just controlling her? And could I stand being with them now, even for a short time, after the uni and a proper, independent existence?'

She told me then about her own family and how 'vanilla' they were – easy going, pretty well off, willing to help her. It all seemed fair enough, and I started to think I was putting up unnecessary obstacles. But I'd got to know her even in the short time we'd been together, and I don't just mean sex. Being – yes, I'll say it – a good-looking and energetic lad, I'd already been round the houses a few times with the sex, enough to know that, unless you're as superficial as a cardboard cut-out, there needs to be more to it.

> *Is she there for you, and you for her,*
> *when the what's it hits the proverbial fan;*
> *will she be fully rounded or a sexual blur*
> *when she turns to woman and you to man?*
> Rob Fuller, aged 18,
> just arrived on campus

Everything she said seemed reasonable and honest, though the whispering in my ear said I wasn't getting the whole story. Still, the project was agreed, and I made my way back to Brookvale Gardens with the agreement of my wonderful Jay. And yes, we talked about new naughties to get up to in our grown-up flat, but we both knew that wasn't really what it was about. We were getting serious about each other.

I couldn't afford a car. A mate gave me a lift to five miles out and I got the bus. As it descended into my home town with Brookvale Gardens on its outskirts, my heart began to sink again.

My last year at Brookvale, A level year, turned pretty grim. Yes, I got a university offer fairly early on, but it needed good grades, and I had no alternative but to slog on more or less all day and every day at Brookvale in order to give myself the chance to get out of it. Apart from the depressing view from my room, I had to field Tony, asking me how it was going and offering any 'study aids' or technological stuff I needed; trying to remain polite to this guy who was where my father should have been tested my patience of itself, never mind all the revision panic, when I realised what notes I hadn't got and what parts of the courses were letting me down.

> *Another quick visit from Mr. Fixit*
> *watching while his stepson bricks it;*
> *benign or vicious, good or bad,*
> *you just ain't never gonna be my dad.*
> Rob Fuller, aged 17, Brookvale Gardens

And, of course, just to add to my confusion, the guy who was my dad wasn't much use either. He phoned regularly, offering 'exam tips' and 'moral support', though my still half-adolescent mind couldn't help thinking that if he was that bothered, he wouldn't have moved seventy miles away. The occasional female voice in the background also suggested there were things he didn't choose to tell his own son.

But as I approached the house, my morale improved. It was a more mature estate now, and it looked it; there were more shops about, the gardens were more developed and varied, and many of the houses had additions, extensions or features front and back.

Mum greeted me with a rather exaggerated enthusiasm, as though she needed to work on it, and I reflected guiltily that, for the last two years that I lived with her, I must have been mostly a pain in the neck. Tony was still on his way home, so it was just the two of us sitting in the new conservatory ten minutes after I arrived. I had to admit to myself the conservatory was nice now that it was finished, spacious, beautifully lit, and full of the plants my mother loved to keep. Then I wondered why I had to 'admit' how good it was. We gazed across at each other in our neat cane armchairs. More than once, people had remarked on how physically similar my mother and I were to each other. We had the same hazel-green eyes, high cheekbones and longish necks. I looked and saw myself older and feminised, and presumably she looked at me and saw herself younger and masculinised. I suppose for some people it would be bizarre or unsettling; we seemed to find it pleasant and oddly comforting.

'I thought maybe I would have a stepbrother or stepsister by now. This is quite a big house for just the two of you'.

I thought articulating one of my secret fears might take the sting out of it.

> *It's not just rejection which I tend to dread*
> *in the morning small hours alone in my bed;*
> *it's having to deal with a brother or sister*
> *begotten by a non-father mister.*
> Rob Fuller, aged 19, in his bedroom on campus

My mother had my sister Jo when she was 20 and me at 22; she was still only 42, which I thought was still on for most women.

'Oh, we like the space', she said. She was looking across at one of her plants, perhaps not doing as well as it should. 'It's a heaven of a house compared to Inkerman Road. In any case, I've been through that twice and that's enough. Apart from that, Tony can't –'

Perhaps it was the plant distraction which had let it slip, but she suddenly gave a guilty start and looked across at me.

'I didn't hear if you didn't want me to hear', I said.

She gazed across at me and then smiled, quickly, like a flashlight.

'Oh, what the hell, Robert. You're a grown man. Just don't tell him you heard it from me'.

A brief silence; someone started up a mower in a garden nearby.

'It destroyed his first marriage, essentially. Yvette thought he'd deliberately concealed it, thinking to rely on her not wanting children; she's a small woman, and there might have been problems. He hadn't concealed it; he genuinely didn't know until they started investigating why it hadn't happened'.

'Oh'.

'Oh? What kind of 'oh' is that, Robert?'

Her eyebrows were down, and I thought maybe I was even more of a pain in my last years in this place than I remembered, and I remembered quite a lot. She had something to say, which seemed to have waited too long for her to keep it suppressed.

'Is that a celebratory 'oh' that the guy who is so inadequate a substitute for your father is so inadequate that he never will be a biological father? Is it an 'oh, as in 'oh, what did you ever see in this man?' Or is it, 'oh, this is your business, he's your bed and you lie on it".

I stood up. I wasn't ready for this, not yet anyway.

'Let's just say it's an 'oh, I've travelled a fair distance and I need a shower'. If you've decided to batter me about, I can at least smell nice'.

She smiled in spite of herself. It's always been my ability to amuse her which has saved things from getting worse between us.

'O.K., darling. Make yourself nice for us. And then you can chat with Tony and I, and tell me the specific reason for your visit. You are a lovely boy, Robert, a good-natured heart-breaker, but you don't do anything without a reason. Mummy loves you, but Mummy doesn't have any illusions'.

> *You're a baby and you watch their eyes melting towards you;*
> *you're a child and you watch their eyes laughing alongside you;*
> *you're a lad and you watch their eyes enjoying your growing*
> *and you realise it isn't just watching, it's knowing.*
> Rob Fuller, aged 20, back in Brookvale Gardens.

After I'd showered, I lingered about in my room with nothing on. I've always liked spending time naked, preferably alone or with a lover; I'm neither flasher nor nudist. It helps me to think, as if the complications disappear with the clothes.

Then I noticed that the full-length mirror which used to be in Jo's room and which I took the mick out of her unmercifully about – ' do you ask it if your bum looks big in it? – seemed to have finished up in mine, suggesting a female guest might have been staying in my room, which made me feel odd. I didn't live here any more, and nothing of me remained other than a few childhood toys or school bits and pieces which Mum didn't want to throw out, but it did bring it home to me that they didn't think that I lived here any more either.

And, of course, I had to look. I don't go in for nude self-examinations a lot, not being a narcissistic kind of guy, but a check-up from time to time makes sense, like having medicals.

But what started as a distracting joke to take my mind off the approaching awkward evening of saying what I wanted and coming to terms with them became something else entirely.

> *Do you ever look to check who you really are?*
> *Stripped of protections, evasions, disguises?*
> *Are you really a dummy who thinks he's a star*
> *feeding on fancies he self-devises?*
> Rob Fuller, aged 20, naked before mirror

I was looking at the entire body of an adult male. Obviously enough male, yes, but let's not go there; let's concentrate, I thought, on the adult bit, the fact that the kid who spent his time in this room has grown up physically and anatomically. But mentally?

What was it, after all, with me and my Mum and Tony? Who in the hell was I to make life miserable for her by taking against the guy she'd chosen? O.K., he wasn't my dad, but where, after all, was my dad? And, more to the point, what was he? A guy who'd never had too much time for me, that's for sure. Or Jo. Or, ultimately, my mother. What his reasons were, I didn't know. But why should I spend the rest of my life disapproving of her making a different choice? And who was I to decide who her choice should be?

Tony wasn't going to stop my pocket money, ground me, tell me what to wear, how to behave. Tony was an adult too, with problems of his own, doing what he could to get by. And Brookvale Gardens? No, it doesn't suit me. But it suits them, and they live here. I don't.

> *What an incredibly tedious game*
> *it would be if we were all the same;*
> *we must choose to be or not to be*
> *but viva a dose of diversity.*
>
> Rob Fuller, aged 21, reflecting on the moments just before his high noon with the 'folks'.

I got dressed quickly, in case I somehow became Narcissus by accident. Then I looked in the mirror at the dressed me. You've done the physical bit, Rob, I said. Do the rest. Grow up.

Downstairs, I kissed my mother and shook hands with Tony. This time, I looked him straight in the eyes and said, 'Hi, Tony. Good to see you again'.

'Hi, Rob', he said. 'You too'. He seemed pleased, if not entirely convinced.

I went straight on, before Mother went into Gestapo mode. Let's get it over with, I thought. They sat on the conservatory sofa, supping glasses of wine. Tony poured me one, and I faced them. My mother's mouth opened, but for once, I got my oar in first.

'Yes, Mum, you're right. I have come back to ask for something. Mercenary me. I'm involved with a girl, as usual; student Casanova, that's me. Except this is a bit different. This is a girl I want to live with and who wants to live with me. In a proper flat, like adults. Away from the University hothouse. We can't buy, and anyway we need to know if it's going to work before we do that. But we still need a deposit, even to rent a flat; we've got some money – we've been saving – but we don't reckon it'll be enough. The area around the University isn't cheap, and there's a lot of competition'.

Mum's mouth was open; Tony was looking at me, but up his nose rather than down it.

I hadn't finished.

'I know you're not my father, Tony, and I know I've been a pain since you two got together. You'd be entirely within your rights to tell me to sod off and wait until I'm working. Though preferably gently. I'll be around anyway, and there will be times, Mum, when I will come back just to see how you are. Honestly. And to introduce you to Jay, of course'.

She had an expression on her face, and I thought the last time she looked at me like that, I was six years old and had given her a bunch of flowers which I'd picked on my way home from school. O.K., I nicked them from the park. It's the thought that counts, isn't it?

Tony was standing up.

'I think we can help, Rob. And in the meantime, why don't we all go out for a meal somewhere? We don't see you very often, and it's nice to make the most of it when we do'.

'Sure'.

We shook hands again. He has an intelligent face, I thought. I'd never noticed before.

I suppose now I should say Jay and I lived happily ever after. Unfortunately, we didn't. The nag in my mind turned out to be that she had already wrapped up the finance with her own parents. Me going to my 'obliging folks' was a test, in effect. And she let me do it even after I'd told her what I'd told her.

'I had to be sure, Rob. You're sweet and beautiful, but you've got a kind of nomad in you, and I wanted to know you'd commit to it'.

We did set up together and yes, the sex was unbelievable;

enough said. But the day came when I discovered the money we'd been putting by sensibly to pay the bills had been ransacked by her to get herself a new outfit for someone's party or whatever. Rows, confrontations, all that stuff. Within weeks, end of.

> *Is it only cynics who resort to laughter*
> *to hear about 'happily ever after'?*
> *No, the chances are you'd find*
> *it's the greater part of humankind.*
> Rob Fuller, aged 23, once more single.

Then, fifteen years ago, I met a lady called Alice. Yes, as in Wonderland. And we have been in something like it ever since, even allowing for bills, mortgages, nappies, sleepless nights, and other things lurking in Wonderland corners. But that's another story. A newer one.

We visited Brookvale Gardens when my son Philip was still a baby, twelve years ago now.

He slept in a cot in my old room, with Alice and I promoted to Jo's old room. Just before going to bed, I went in to check the listening alarm. He was fast asleep, snoozing happily.

'I coped, son. You obviously can too. That's my boy'.

> *Whatever I've done, whatever I did,*
> *can't match the sight of my sleeping kid;*
> *the envy, the boredom, the living Big Dipper,*
> *have all met their match in my little nipper.*
> Rob Fuller, aged 28, Dad.

BEING DESDEMONA

The main two happenings in my life on that day in 1990 were the annual school swimming gala and an evening entirely given over to yet another reading through of my part as Desdemona in the ambitious sixth form production of Othello. The posters were up all over the school – CLARE FOWLER as Desdemona, the letters nearly as big as Othello and Iago. A stage career was my target at the time, and after some parts in school and drama group productions, I auditioned and got the female lead in the play. But I was also doing three A levels, and keeping all my plates balanced in the air was proving difficult. I'd thought of withdrawing from the play, but the director was a teacher, Mrs. Elizabeth Nicholson, universally known as Beth, who'd directed me in three previous productions. Nit-picking and punctilious as she was, she deserved more than one of her principals letting her down in the final build-up.

The afternoon gala was pressure off playtime, for non-competitors, anyway. I'd never been more than an indifferent swimmer and was once again wedged amongst a group of us intent on talent-spotting the boys and bitching about the girls.

'She's going to have to have those lifted before she's twenty, I reckon'.

'Look at him, the one with the python in his pants!'

Yes, I know, but we were working hard and we needed occasional silliness – being big kids, which is what we were, when all's said and done. All of us had been on the receiving end at being ogled at the gala one time or another. My house team had been so hit by flu absence in Year 9 that I'd been dragooned into a race, and I could well remember those rows and rows of eyes beamed directly at skinny, half naked little me.

And, in any case, Desdemona was so on my mind that I couldn't stop thinking about her.

The play's three night run was ten days away, and I still had trouble understanding the woman. I took very seriously the process of thinking my way right into the part. This young woman who had the self-assertiveness to actually fancy and marry a black man in an intensely racist and macho society doesn't have the gumption to sort out that a transparent baddie like Iago is poisoning her husband against her, and when said husband makes himself her judge and jury and decides to do away with her, instead of pronouncing firmly, 'do you hell as like, buster' and whacking him with a rolling pin, she languishes palely about on the bed saying 'oh, please, lord and master, I am innocent, please don't harm fragile little me', or words to that effect. I felt that Desdemona showed the kind of virtuous helplessness that would have Germaine Greer shaking her head in despair and expounding about how English literature, by men and for men, perpetuates the stereotypes generation after generation.

The steam in my mind was rising as hotly as the steam in the great echoing space of the baths, and at that moment, the sixth form lads emerged to take part in their race, amongst them a handsome black boy called John Waite. None of us had ever seen John Waite so naked and so close – we were only thirty yards from the starting blocks – and the poor boy took off his gown to a kind of collective gasp from the ranks.

'Legs all the way up to his bum!'

'Take me out and fan me; I've got a flush coming on!'

I will not descend into the schoolkid lewdness which many of us, boys and girls, indulged in on Gala day. Enough to say that John Waite was a sight to behold. He wasn't the body builder, muscle bound type; he was long and sleek, and his legs were so smooth and shaped as to be almost feminine, but the square, sculptured shoulders and the perfection of the six pack would have graced a Michelangelo statue.

I well imagined that I could fall in love with John Waite just because of his beauty, even though I knew very little about him. He was sporty, of course, not just swimming, but basketball, cricket, what have you, and I think he was about to exhibit work on the Art A level course, which suggested an interesting combination of talents. He seemed a pleasant, easy-going character from the few times I'd spoke to him, with none of the surly arrogance of one or two of the other sporting stars of the school. Even now, he didn't seem at all aware of the effect he was having on the ranks of girls. Some of his bending and twisting exercises were stretching a few eyes even wider. A friend nearby, Jane Cooper, had her mouth open and her eyebrows seemed to have almost disappeared into her hair; her neighbour Rosie Gordon had her mouth in a perfect O.

'Close your gob, Jane, before rigor mortis sets in!'

'Rosie, darling, your knuckles have gone white!'

But then, like a sudden douche of cold water, I thought of Desdemona again, as the question banged repeatedly in my mind like a clattering door in the wind – would I actually really dare to go out with John Waite? How would some of John's classmates react to the two of us chatting amicably in the corner of the Common Room? We all told ourselves, in the liberated days of 1990, that prejudice didn't exist any more, but it did and, let's be honest about it, it still does. Whose eyes would be flickering across at us, and what would be in those looks?

'Clare likes to take a walk on the wild side, doesn't she?'

'If it moves and shaves, she'll give it a try'.

How long would it be before I'd be driven to lose my temper by the giggling comments which flash around the changing rooms and the girls' loos?

'Come on, Clare, legends about black boys, true or not?'

'Is he sizing up, Clare? Proving a bit much for you?'

Race riots had disfigured Britain all through the eighties. In the weekend pubs and clubs, in the late night haze of too much drink, long taxi queues, crowds of boys and crowds of girls, how would things go when John and I missed our taxi and had to walk it? Perhaps a little group collected on the pavement at three a.m. with John and I at the centre of it.

'If you're that desperate, darling, we'll have to help you out'.

'Let's see if Sambo really is a big tough guy'.

And I thought of my own parents, both avowedly liberal and unprejudiced people; what would I see in **their** eyes when I brought John home for dinner? Is it still about Guess Who's Coming to Dinner? Would it be real indifference to his colour, or the kind of euphemisms people used when reacting to inter-racial experiences?

'I'm no racist, Clare, as you know well enough, but there will always be snags in such relationships. We have to face the fact that the world isn't always as we'd want it to be'.

'The whole gender thing is pretty difficult to start with, Clare; when it's cultures and attitudes which have to find a meeting place as well as male and female, it isn't easy'.

And I would ridicule their hide-bound attitudes, no doubt, and of course John Waite is undoubtedly as English as I am, but what about **his** parents? Would they have a liberality and an open-mindedness that would put mine to shame? What would they interpret as the role of a wife? And what would John himself understand to be the role of a wife?

'It's understood that the men do the bread-winning, Clare, and the women the bread-making; that's how my Gran would put it, and I don't argue with her, let me tell you'.

'If you work full-time, Clare, you will shame me before my family'.

Desdemona, of course, in her time, would have gone through all this and worse, gentle born as she was, for the sake of her love, and for as long as Othello was the flavour of the month and the successful general the politicians needed, she would have been able to ignore the mutterings. But Othello was a soldier, and Desdemona must have known there were at least two big risks associated with that; one, he could be killed in battle, leaving her effectively without protection; two, he could lose a battle, or even a war, and she could finish up paying the price he paid, or worse.

'Whatever you thought you were, my lady, all you are now is the ex-concubine of a Moor. Look not for mercy from your own people when your lust has betrayed them'.

'Your family, madam, have nothing to say. Their silence is more eloquent than your words'. Exactly what happened to widows of inter-racial marriages in those days I didn't know, but some of their other practices suggested it could be pretty bad. Desdemona would have known that as well.

John Waite didn't win his race, but he won the biggest cheer when he emerged from the water, the hair sleeked right back and the trunks even tighter. He stood momentarily beside the pool, shaking water from him, and he was a Hockney painting, a Da Vinci angel.

I screamed and hollered along, partly for the fun of the day, but partly because I'd just got it with Desdemona. She had decided to place her entire life with him, every last ounce of courage, self-assertion, honesty and feeling she possessed, and when the whole thing came crashing down around her ears, she just didn't want to go on. She had no strength left. She gambled it all and lost it all.

And so it must be true, that what you are giving is not necessarily going to be renewed or re-born; what you are giving might be all of it, so much so that, once it's gone, there's nothing left. If the amount and power of what you're giving is as great as Desdemona's offering, the emptiness is all the more devastating.

The performances went well. I understood now and I could relate to it fully. Othello was a blacked-up boy called Will Syerson. I thought the make-up was ridiculous and I couldn't help wondering what John Waite must have thought; I knew he would go to see it on one night, almost everyone in the sixth form did. Will didn't look like a general, but he was a very good actor – he went professional later – and we worked together so well that when we got to the big murder scene on the last night, we were in tears and so were half of the audience.

As it turned out, that was the swan song of my professional acting ambitions, though not the end of my acting; I continued as an amateur and avoided leading parts. I was so shattered by the physical and mental effort that I thought doing it for a living, night after night, would burn me out very soon, even assuming I stayed in employment. I married a teacher like myself, an intelligent, sexy, deeply honest man and the whole thing became blessedly simple when I realised that I **had** fallen in love with him. But, even now, I still can't really say whether I would have dared to fall in love with John Waite. Thirty years on, as a woman marching undaunted through her forties, with a formidable, if amateur, collection of productions in my past, I reflect on the progress we've made, both since Desdemona's days and since 1990. No, we don't take decisions, personal or public, on the grounds of race any more. No, we don't follow people with racist notions any more. Do we?

YEARNING TO BREATHE FREE

THE FOURNIER BAKERY, RUE DU FAUBOURG-SAINT-MARTIN, PARIS – WEDNESDAY JUNE 17TH 1778

There were times, Claudette thought, when the Fournier bakery resembled her picture of Hell itself; dark, extremely hot and full of potentially damaging equipment. Her husband, Fournier himself, from a family so steeped in bakery it was named after an oven, was sweating and cursing alongside his eldest son Pierre, and at the moment it was men's muscle that was needed to deal with and shape the heavy dough. She asked little from squat, strong-armed balding Fournier – everyone, including her, called him Fournier, or Monsieur Fournier if they were on the make – but this particular brief breather was one of her few perks.

The street outside was almost as hot and smelt worse, but an occasional waft of breeze was better than nothing. She sat down on the little stool she took with her from the shop, and almost immediately, two boys suddenly appeared from a nearby side street running towards her as if their lives depended on it.

This didn't bother her at all; boys dashing about was nothing unusual. But they were soon close enough for her to see that the one on the left was her youngest son Henri, aged ten, and both his and his companion's eyes were wild with panic and fear. She got up from her stool. He and his friend had no sooner burst past her into the shop when seven men also appeared from the same street and started running towards her at full speed.

She moved rapidly back into the shop and closed the door. So much for her short break and breath of air, she thought, and little Henri was going to need to have a very good tale to tell if she wasn't to take a stick to his skinny rear.

'Hide us, Maman, please, please –' the boy said. He was almost in tears, and this was very rare for Henri, as tough a pup as could be, able to hold his own with all the local boys, though hardly tall, even for his age.

'I would be very grateful for your protection, Madame', said the other boy; his careful accent and his odd clothes suddenly made her aware of him. But the men's thundering boots were coming ever nearer, and Claudette Fournier could think and act quickly when the need arose. She hurried the boys down to the cellar, bolting doors behind her on the way. In the dim light of the cellar store room, they listened to the men clattering on past and their bursts of language blistered Claudette's ears, used as she was to men's talk.

'Now, Henri, what is all this about? This had better be good. And who is your friend?'

They had both managed to calm their panic quite well by now, but Henri still took another deep breath before replying.

'Maman, this is Marcel, son of the Comte de Sevres'.

Momentarily struck dumb, Claudette now looked properly at the boy. Yes, of course; the snooty gait, for all his recent exercise, the front foot elegantly pushed forward, and the clothes simply wrong. Henri was no street urchin; she kept him as decently clothed as her means allowed, but even without the gaudy decorations and fineries, the Comte's son was clad in cloth way beyond what a baker's family could afford. Anger suddenly elbowed anxiety away, and Claudette seized a long stick from one of the firewood stacks nearby.

'I haven't got time for this', she said. 'Henri, what on earth have you done to cause a whole group of grown men to come chasing after you like maniacs? Tell me, boy, and tell me the truth, because if you have endangered yourself or this family, I will have to beat you long and hard to impress upon you to be more careful. I may not be able to punish his little lordship here, but I can give you enough for the two of you –'

'I can take my share, Madame, if I need to', Marcel said slowly. 'When my father decides I need a whipping, which he rarely does – he is a dutiful father, but he is not a cruel man – he has a burly fellow for the purpose, and it might well be my fate when I get home today'.

They both stood there, their eyes still wild and wide from their experience, Henri's hazel brown, lively and intelligent, and the little Comte's a startling ice blue, signalling defiance and independence.

Claudette opened her mouth, but the aristo whelp hadn't finished.

'I simply want to understand my people, Madame. Everyone in this street is living on my family's land. My father is sickly and, much as it grieves and worries me, it is possible I will all too soon be the Comte de Sevres myself. I live my life in a cage – a luxurious cage, yes, with all possible comforts and tutors provided for my education – but a cage nevertheless. If I am to look after people who will be my tenants and servants, I want to know something of them and their world, or how else can I do the job entrusted to me by Providence?'

'Very good, Monsieur, but where does my Henri come into it?'

Henri, of course, had been quiet for far too long.

'Marcel and I got talking when his coach had slipped a wheel turning at the end of the street. He was sitting nearby while it was mended, watched over by one of his men, and he saw me looking at him in all his gaudy finery. He beckoned me, and waved his man back. 'All I ever see is the inside of coaches, the inside of rooms', he said. 'I want to know what is happening, how people live. If I disguise myself, will you run with me sometimes?' I said I will if you do what I tell you to do and, above all, keep quiet; you are an aristo as soon as you open your mouth. The next thing I know, we are standing near a café and listening to a group of men talking freely about overthrowing the King and setting up a republic. Suddenly, Marcel is almost shouting at them about being traitors to France and his father will have them all arrested. I managed to get him on his feet and away before the men got into their stride, or I can't imagine what would have happened to us'.

'Perhaps I deserve to be whipped for sheer stupidity', Marcel said.

'Perhaps', Henri said, looking at his friend. 'But how long I would have lasted in your world, Marcel, without making a mistake, I couldn't say'.

'Is it so wrong for us to be friends, Madame?' Marcel said. Claudette looked at the eyes again, so young, so alive, and her girlhood running free in the Norman countryside, in and out of the trees and tracks, came vividly back to her. Her anger eased, and her practical side asserted itself – a son befriending the heir of an aristo was not an opportunity to be easily spurned. If this boy would one day, perhaps one day not far into the future, have the power of tenancy or eviction in his hands, a certain amount of friendly acquaintance could be very useful; some friendships formed in childhood lasted a lifetime.

'No, Monsieur, there is never much wrong with friendship. But true friends try to avoid getting their friends into trouble, not drag them into it. If you are to run with Henri, as you call it, you must remember what he tells you; keep quiet, pretend to be a deaf mute or something, keep away from places where men gather and drink, and don't forget that Henri has duties of his own and doesn't have unlimited time to run the streets'.

'Thank you, Maman', Henri said, and the brown eyes were glistening now. She gathered both of them into her. Henri was the youngest of the five children to survive her ten pregnancies, and the survivors all had such a place in her heart that she could never stay angry with them for long, especially the youngest.

'But what to do now?' she said, as their little group hug broke up. She was still holding the stick, absurdly, and she threw it briskly back into the woodpile. She thought for a moment.

'Henri is not too badly off for clothes; he has two older brothers and he is much the same size as they were at his age. If you go with him again, Marcel, you will find a quiet spot near the Sevres town house, put on what he brings you and change back when you leave him. For today, I will get Jean-Claude to take you in the delivery cart with a cover over you – he knows all the quiet routes – to the neighbourhood of the Sevres house. You could tell your father you were meeting a friend and you got lost. If your father is as you say he is, I doubt whether that is a sin worthy of a whipping, but if it should prove to be, then you are to consider, Marcel, as we humble folk have to every day of our lives, that actions have consequences'.

For the first time, Marcel looked a little embarrassed, even ashamed.

'As you are so good, Madame, I must be honest, and there is not much risk on this occasion. My father is at his sanatorium and will not be back until this evening, and the burly fellow is not an informer. I don't doubt you're right, Madame, but I am safe for today at least'.

They were interrupted by a sound of such ill-tempered rage that all three of them jumped involuntarily, even in the protection of their cellar.

'Claudette, where the HELL are you?' Fournier's indignation knew no bounds when any family member wasn't doing exactly what Fournier wanted them to do. Claudette's grace and favour break was well and truly at an end. The knot of anxiety that gnawed away at her about Fournier twisted again; Fournier was not violent, or not towards her at least, though the boys had been on the receiving end often enough, but he was ageing quickly and this exhausting intemperance of his worried her.

'Stay here, both of you. I will send Jean-Claude down to you and you can leave through the back gate, Marcel under cover. Jean-Claude is a good servant who doesn't ask questions; bless him, he probably wouldn't understand the answers in any case'.

'Good God, woman, have you walked out on me? In the middle of a working day? CLAUDETTE!'

She kissed each small forehead and gave them both an arch look which set them giggling. That's more like it, she thought as she climbed the stairs; that's the kind of noise children ought to be making.

FOURNIER BAKERY, SATURDAY APRIL 25TH 1789

The clamour outside was mounting, and Claudette was standing in the stock room behind the main shop, with two burly sons on either side of her, Pierre on her right and Georges on her left. They had both left boyhood well behind and they were big men, with Fournier's build but height more typical of her own Norman d'Avranches family, who had wanted more for her than angry little Fournier. But Fournier was, after all, a businessman in Paris, with more money potential than any of the small-scale Norman shops in Caen.

Fournier himself was no more, having flown into a tantrum once too often in 1786, his heart finally giving up on sustaining a man irate almost from sunrise to sunset. And Henri, her jewel, with more brains and initiative than all her other children put together, had decided that sweating away in a city bakery was not for him and the only way he could see the world was in the Army. It was over six months since Claudette had heard from him, and as that was from a barracks in France, she couldn't understand why he was unable to get in contact or visit or do something.

Thank goodness, she thought, as a lump of jagged wood splintered one of the smaller side windows, that Mireille and Esme had been successfully, if not particularly profitably, married off; delicate Esme would never have been able to deal with this, and Mireille would have launched herself into some foolishness which would have made the situation worse.

'If you can't make bread we can afford', a coarse voice sounded through the broken window, followed by expressions which made even a woman of the world like Claudette shudder, 'we'll make sure you can't make any bread at all, you bitch!'

I can only make as much bread as the available grain allows me to make, Claudette thought, though she remained too terrified to utter it. She was quite determined not to adulterate the bread with the appalling rubbish and street-sweepings that some put in it to make it seem more, and cheap. Grain was more and more expensive after another poor harvest, so the prices had to be passed on. She was running a business, not a charity.

But the mob no longer cared. She knew quite a few of the insane crowd now surging around the front of the shop, and it hurt her to see old friends and neighbours running with the mob, too frightened to argue or defend her business.

A huge crash against the front door forced her to a decision.

'The cellar, boys, now, down to the cellar!'

Pierre, bread knife in one hand and rolling pin in the other, looked at her reproachfully.

'Maman, can we not at least –'

'No, Pierre, we cannot. They are a mob; they are insane and fighting them might cost you your life. A bakery is not worth your life; the cellar, please, and you too, Georges –'

She nudged and pushed at Georges who seemed frozen with terror, but it took Pierre's more determined shove to move him. Picking up the weeping Jean-Claude from the grain store, stark as it was, they clattered away even as the mob broke in and started looting what little stores of bread she had managed to hold in reserve. Down, down, down, locking every door after them and hoping against hope none of the mob had found their way down to the little alley which the cellar opened onto. Down to the very spot where, nearly eleven years ago, she had had her one and only close up contact with a bona fide member of the French aristocracy, who she knew had succeeded his father as Comte de Sevres in 1783. While he was a huge improvement on some of the landlords known in her area of Paris, he kept mostly to the Sevres town house and the Sevres chateau miles away in the Vendee, his childish follies now dismissed as such in his mind, no doubt. This time there was no leisure to stand and talk; they were through the door into the mercifully empty alley and shortly enmeshed in the maze of back alleys passing behind the shops and counting houses of the Rue du Faubourg.

By the time they found their way back onto the main street, a good six hundred *pieds du roi* up from their shop front, they looked down to their left at the diminishing mob outside, with all those who had found any bread, or even bread ingredients, scampering away with them before anyone could stop them. Then a gathering pall of smoke rose from the shop.

'Oh my God, they are burning it down', said Claudette, retreating into the alley and finally bending her head to weep, as her two boys consoled her and Jean-Claude sank to the ground with his head in his hands.

For once, Georges had a moment of his own. He was the first to see, way down at the far end of the street, a grand coach begin its rapid progress towards them, relying on anyone in their way to get out of it rapidly. They all knew the Sevres coat of arms and the Sevres livery clearly enough. Two men were perched on the front of the coach, one of them armed, and a further two at the back were also armed. Two more guns were emerging from inside the coach, one of them clearly held by the young Comte de Sevres himself, now an athletically built and immaculately dressed and wigged young man. As if that was not discouragement enough for the rapidly dispersing mob, the coach was followed by a group of six horsemen, and as Claudette looked and looked again, her heart almost stopped at the realisation that the one at the front was undoubtedly her Henri, showing the superb horsemanship the Army had taught him. He blew her a kiss and waved to his brothers as he thundered on past.

Claudette and the three young men with her abandoned all caution and went pelting down the street after the mounted men. By the time they reached the front of the bakery, it was clear that the shop and parts of the wooden buildings behind it were already beyond saving. The Sevres men were concentrating on getting what water they could from the drainage trenches running down the street and the surrounding shops to help the neighbouring traders stop the fire before it engulfed the whole street.

For some hours, all was chaos and confusion; Sevres' following and Henri and his men helped the desperate locals fight the fire and some help eventually turned up from the Parisian authorities, which some declared, if quietly, was a miracle in itself. A few brave souls who had an idea of continuing looting were briskly discouraged by gunfire. It went on and on and on, and at the end of it, an exhausted, bedraggled and smoke-blackened Claudette found herself being gently helped up into the Sevres coach.

'Your servant, Madame', said the Comte, and his gorgeous gold and blue clothing was bespattered with dirt and even singed in parts. Even his wig was decidedly askew, but the face and those ice-blue eyes related back only too clearly to the little boy who had once stood forlornly, if proudly, in her own cellar.

'Marcel – may I call you Marcel, Monsieur le Comte?'

'Of course you may, Madame; perhaps I may even take the liberty of calling you Claudette?' She nodded. 'Henri alerted me to how things were; he had only just come back from his leave when he heard rumours about the ugly mood in Paris, particularly directed at the supposedly profiteering bakers –'

'I can't make bread without grain, Mon – er – Marcel. Not proper bread, which isn't going to poison people. But where is Henri? I have yet to have the chance to speak to him. And why is he here at all –'

A sudden noise outside, and then he was there, Henri himself, climbing into the coach while his brothers and poor Jean-Claude, weeping quietly, waited deferentially outside. Claudette had her arms around her youngest boy once again; she felt the strength and power of him, and her despair began to ebb away, even as the remains of her business smouldered.

'I got indefinite leave, Maman', he said. 'Most of us have not been paid for months anyway – the Army is falling apart between the royalists and the revolutionaries – and the boys who came with me also have relatives in this city which seems to be slowly going out of its mind. I was sure Marcel would help, even after all this time'.

Outside, Claudette saw Jean Claude being helped up on to the back of the coach, and Pierre and Georges sharing some of the men's horses. She felt the sensation of movement as the coach trotted away more sedately than it had arrived. She turned to look at the count.

'As your son says, Claudette, Paris is mad and dangerous, and it is best for us to make the whole trip to the Chateau de Sevres to consider the future. We are a large and well-armed enough party to look after ourselves. You will be my guests until the decisions we need to take are taken, and I am only too desolate not to have arrived early enough to save your business, Madame Claudette. You may rely on me to make amends'.

As the fetid Paris air gave way to the fresher country breezes, Claudette felt her eyes closing and her head drooping. A nightmare had turned into a dream, and it was time to rest.

WEDNESDAY OCTOBER 23RD 1793 – RUE DU FAUBOURG-SAINT-MARTIN

The tumbril turned into the street, with four armed soldiers leading it and two others following. Robespierre considered it amusing to send the Comte de Sevres through the heart of his own Parisian possessions on his way to the guillotine. Robespierre couldn't know then that his own time would soon come, and his supposed incorruptibility did not stop him from enjoying what he saw as his own little jokes.

The Comte de Sevres himself was standing at the very front of the cart. He had been considered important enough to have a tumbril to himself, typical of the Committee's ambiguous attitude to the leading aristos. Though his only clothes were breeches and a thin open neck shirt and his rather gaunt face had paled considerably, there was nothing in his manner to suggest fear or despair. People near to the tumbril noticed the undimmed ice blue eyes glancing around at the territory he knew so well. Like many aristos, he had been taught from an early age not to display naked emotion, and his mental resistance to what was happening to him was boosted by the absurdity of it; he was a vigorous, well-made twenty five year old man with a promising future, quite possibly in public service, and the nonsensical charges laid against him were unfounded and unproven. Yes, he had many royalist friends – most of his schoolmates had been royalists – and yes, he had and did correspond with them. It was hardly surprising, given the chaos that France had become, that the state of the country had been mentioned more than once. But to say it amounted to plotting against the revolution was ridiculous, given that most of it was before the Revolution was even seen as a vague possibility.

As the tumbril clattered sedately down the street – Robespierre felt that people should have time to look at the condemned and see for themselves the consequences of defiance – the escorting soldiers became more restless with each passing step. They had become used to people's hostility, or more usually by now, indifference to prisoners going to their graves, but it was rapidly becoming clear that the atmosphere here was very different. People were emerging from their shops and houses, and the murmuring gradually increased in volume to something like the growls of a pack of animals. Sevres had restored the street at his own expense after the fires and riots three years ago, and unlike many of his class, fleeing Paris and even the country at the first available opportunity, he had stayed to try to protect his own people from the excesses of the regime.

Sevres found himself smiling at the people he knew. I did everything, he was thinking, everything I could humanly do to keep myself alive; I even had the good fortune to fall in love and marry Francoise Bertillon, the daughter of one of the leading lawyers backing the Revolution; such highly placed contacts as this made available should have protected him for long enough to keep him and his people safe. But his intense, instinctive personal dislike of Robespierre and Francoise's outspoken self – beautiful, big-eyed and brunette she was, diplomatic she wasn't – had ultimately brought him to this. He didn't even know where Francoise was; he hadn't seen her since his arrest, and for all he knew she might already be dead, with their first child still inside her; the Revolution spared no-one, even unborn babies. It was as black as it could possibly be, but his father and his teachers had taught him that the blackest times demanded the bravest men, and he was still the Comte de Sevres.

The leading soldiers saw that the other end of the street was closing to them with the sheer volume of people placing themselves in front and around the tumbril. The officer in charge ordered the tumbril's driver to accelerate his horse, but the mounting noise was upsetting the animal.

As the tumbril forced its way uneasily past the restored Fournier bakery, everything happened simultaneously. Eight men, led by the three Fournier brothers, suddenly emerged from a nearby alley; Claudette herself came out from her shop, accompanied by Francoise Bertillon, no longer in hiding, and they nodded signals at people up and down the street. The people moved in to surround the soldiers and prevent them from having room enough to use their weapons; the Fournier brothers and their friends smashed the back gate of the tumbril and helped Sevres down. Before the soldiers could fire a shot, the Comte had been hurried away down the alley from which the Fournier brothers and their friends had emerged and within minutes, everyone had discreetly disappeared, the horse had bolted, dragging the wrecked tumbril behind it, and six bewildered and bedraggled soldiers found themselves alone, gazing about them with the air of abandoned children.

WEDNESDAY NOVEMBER 6TH 1793, CHATEAU DE SEVRES, NEAR LES EPESSES IN THE VENDEE REGION OF FRANCE, 280 MILES SOUTH WEST OF PARIS.

The main salon of the house gave onto a magnificent stone balcony looking over the splendid Vendee countryside. Marcel had not often been allowed here as a boy, his father regarding it as adult territory, and the fact that he now owned it and could use it to his heart's content gave him an inordinate amount of pleasure. The day was autumnal, with a stiff northern breeze making its presence felt, but he and his wife had matters of great moment to discuss and neither of them had any doubts about the ability of servants to eavesdrop if they chose to do so.

'Yes, Marcel, we are safe here', Francoise said, leaning towards him, her dark eyes wider than ever and her very physical presence exciting him, as it always did. 'I knew when Henri told me what he had in mind that this was the safest place for us; he urged me to trust him and I did. For the moment, the whole Vendee has risen against the Revolution and it would take an entire army for them to prise us out of here'.

He forced himself to be rational; not easy, with her flushed beauty at such proximity.

'Yes, that's true. But it cannot last. The Vendee cannot conquer the rest of France unless the country rises up with them, and it will not. The Vendee might want to restore the idiotic Bourbon monarchy; no-one else does. Paris will soon send armies big enough to crush the Vendee, and then the retributions will be terrible indeed'.

She registered a gesture of exasperation, but she knew he was right.

'Henri thinks we should go to America, all of us', Marcel said.

'America?' She said the word as if she had never heard it before. She gazed at him in amazement.

'You, an aristocrat with blood ties to the King of France, would go to a country which has just successfully rebelled against its king? Do you think they will welcome you?'

Marcel moved towards the front wall of the balcony and gazed down over his land.

'They were happy enough to accept help from the French monarchy to win their independence. Some people think that war caused the Revolution; France bankrupted itself helping the Americans break free of the British and hadn't got enough resources left to feed and house its own people. They were also happy enough to take the assistance of a French aristocrat, the Marquis de Lafayette. They are a new, young country, needing and welcoming immigrants, and looking to build a future rather than fight the same old battles over again. The choice for those who stay in France is between a murderous tyranny which has slaughtered thousands of its own people in cold blood, and an inept monarchy which keeps itself in the lap of luxury while its people starve'.

'Yes, there is much in what you say, my darling'. Francoise considered the practicalities, as she tended to do. 'We could sell everything; there is no shortage of local worthies who would want to get their hands on this chateau. We could charter a ship out of La Rochelle; there are enough standing idle at the moment. We sail far enough south to keep out of the way of the British Navy, and we make sure our ship is fast and has guns'.

Now she was on her feet, her whole being active and involved, and he loved her all over again. A discreet tap on the windows behind them; Henri Fournier stood there, now Master of the Sevres horse, gazing a little nervously out. Marcel went and flung the doors open.

'You will catch your death, Monsieur Le Comte, out here in the November wind'. He smiled.

'When we get to the United States of America, Henri, you really must stop calling me that'.

'You mean – '

'Yes, darling Henri, we do mean', said Francoise, and for a moment, they looked at each other like three wild children contemplating the naughtiest prank imaginable. Then Henri's face was suddenly disconsolate.

'My mother will not go. Neither will Pierre and Georges. I have sounded them all out about it. We know it is still too dangerous to go back to Paris. My mother wants to go back to her parents in Caen and help them run the Auberge d'Avranches; they are trying to run it on their own now, and her father is not well at all. This is the world they know, Marcel, and they will not abandon it, however difficult it might be'.

'And they will have my help, Henri, at the very least with the passage there, which will need organisation and support in the teeth of this remorseless fighting. But does that stop you?'

A long, long pause, as Henri gazed at his feet, and then at the view over Sevres country, and then at his two companions. His back straightened and his face set.

'No', he said, quietly but firmly. 'I love France, and I hope one day to return, when the poor country has done with its desperate turmoil, at least for a while. But I need something different; I need to live without bowing and scraping to every arrogant fool with a title – forgive me, Marcel, but you are not typical, by any means – and above all, I need a chance to make a life away from this endless, pointless bloodshed'.

In the silence following his words, a stiffening breeze brought them the sounds of the Sevres estate stretching out below them to the very horizon; the plod of horses drawing their ploughs; somewhere, the buzz of playing children; the clunking of carts along makeshift roads and, mercifully distant but nevertheless audible, the spasmodic dull thud of cannons.

THURSDAY APRIL 18TH 2019, RESTAURANT CHEZ FOURNIER, RUE DU FAUBOUG-SAINT-MARTIN

Anthony J. Sevren, attorney at law, a slim, well-dressed man with an easy authoritative air and disconcerting ice-blue eyes, and John Furness, archivist and historian, more casually clothed and more academic and detached, had just enjoyed a three course Parisian dinner and were at their ease on the terrace outside the restaurant, enjoying two glasses of very old Calvados and watching the evening strollers pass up and down in front of them.

'I had to pull in a favour or two to get this trip at all, John, I don't mind telling you. But I'm glad I did. Ever since you got in touch with me last year, I've felt the whole fog of my family history has been lifted and I can feel – connected, I suppose, is the word'.

'Yes, and that's good to know, because that's a lot of what I'm trying to do. Families might spread themselves all over places and time, but the roots business is as it ever was'.

'So we know that Claudette did come back, judging by the name of this place?'

'She did. In 1800, well after the Terror had subsided, Claudette and her sons moved back to her bakery. Both of her parents had died by then, and the Auberge d'Avranches taken over by her cousins. She'd been sending Pierre on regular trips to check up on the situation in Paris, and by 1800 they felt safe enough to go back. The case against Sevres collapsed, in any case, after Robespierre's death, and the fact that she and her family had helped Sevres to escape was more in their favour than against them. Exactly when the bakery turned into a restaurant we don't know, since for a while it seemed to function as both, but Pierre Fournier's grandson Michel proved an artist at cooking generally as well as baking, and that swung it towards the restaurant'.

'But Henri never went back?'

'No, he didn't, which is sad, I suppose, but it wouldn't have been feasible while the Naploeonic Wars continued, and in 1812, of course, Britain and the U.S. were at war for a while. He couldn't possibly have returned before 1816, and by then Henri was 48 and not too well, with a family of his own to look after. Oddly enough, considering his youthful aversion to it, he set up as a baker, with Marcel's help initially, your great many times over grandfather, but as an American baker; by the turn of the century, he had twenty shops, and by 1816, over fifty. He didn't get back to see Claudette before she died in 1817. Henri himself died in 1836, and it was his grandson Philippe who anglicised the name to Furness in 1866 after the Civil War, when everyone with an un-American name was seen as suspicious'.

'And Marcel the Comte, my noble ancestor, prospered in the States?'

'Yes, he did. He bought an estate near Boston, and staffed it with a mixture of American people and French emigres – not all the people who fled France back then were aristocrats; in fact, only a minority of them were. Francoise adapted her knowledge of law to the American codes and made herself legally useful to both American and French clients, so they did well enough for themselves and started the dynastic legal tradition which continues in you, Anthony. Exactly when they anglicised the name by changing one letter of it, we don't know, but Marcel's grandson Hugh was a precise, fussy man and we think it was probably him, to stop himself from having to keep on pronouncing the name to people'.

They fell quiet and sipped their drinks, watching the remorseless drift of passing people, whose racial and ethnic diversity was very obvious.

'They're coming here now, John, aren't they?'

'Who?'

'The huddled masses of Emma Lazarus. 'Your huddled masses yearning to breathe free'. They were all ours once, and now here they are in Europe, and thirty years down the line, who's going to have the ageing population and more sick old people than people of working age, and who's going to have a more youthful population and a more diverse and adaptable culture? We gained from the English religious wars and the French revolutionary wars, and now the tide flows away from us rather than to us. Welcome to the New World, John'.

WORD OF MOUTH

Pulling back the curtains revealed a gun-metal grey day, the leaves scudding wildly on the pavements below; a physically depressing morning to follow a mentally depressing evening of disturbing local news and addressing the gaps in his A level revision. However, Rob persuaded himself out of bed and into his running gear, as he did most mornings. Kate, A levels, running – so far, he was still balancing all his plates in the air and aimed to stay that way, whatever was happening in his home town.

Daniel, ten years old and unconcerned about hiding his liking for school, had his books already laid out on the kitchen table to prepare for the day. Rob's brother's impish, unaffected smile greeted him as it always did, though Daniel also seemed worried about the town news. Rob fixed his eyes on the boy's face so he could read the lips, which they both generally found easier than sign language, though they could do it.

'Are you sure you should, Rob? With this stuff going on?' Daniel mouthed, and then he nodded at the edition of the local paper still laying on the kitchen table. Rob knew what his brother meant. At the bottom of the cliffs in the coastal town where they lived, the body of a young woman, reputedly not much older than a girl, had been found only five days ago. Although fully clothed, she didn't seem to have any identifying documents or possessions on her at all, and the report said that being bumped about over the rocks and under the water would have made the body unrecognisable. The police had no missing girl reports, and though local opinion had already decided on a suicide – it happened along the cliffs, though mercifully rarely – the police didn't seem happy with that theory, and were known to still be investigating.

'I can't put my life on hold for one mysterious incident, Dan, especially as it maybe wasn't all that mysterious. I'll be careful; I always am. See you later'.

Daniel grinned again, a grin infectious enough to leave Rob smiling as he started out. Predictably in view of the grey sky, the first drops started to fall within minutes. Profoundly deaf, a specialist had described Daniel as, but essentially he was a good kid and he didn't let it get him down. As the rain thickened, Rob's smile faded and the temptation to replace the run with a hot shower and breakfast was very powerful, but he was no stranger to difficult coastal weather and he soon established his usual easy rhythm. He was representing his athletics club in a prestigious race in less than two weeks and top form was needed, rain or no rain.

By Harbour Road, the downpour had become relentless. Rob shook rain from his eyes and hair and watched where his feet were landing; late April was already the tourist season here, with dangerous debris sometimes on the pavements. An ankle turned, a muscle pulled in an avoiding twist, could put him out of running, possibly for weeks.

He pattered on down Harbour Road, ready to turn down towards the beach at the end of it. This was a less salubrious part of town; one or two of the B and Bs were widely reputed to be involved in less respectable activities, and the section of cliff above where the girl's body had been found was just a few minutes' run away. Rob determined to be as alert as possible.

But a sudden loud tapping at a window across the road nevertheless startled him enough for his foot to connect awkwardly with a beer can, sending him spinning across the road clutching at his foot like a Charlie Chaplin impersonator. His natural athleticism seemed to have prevented any damage other than a slight soreness; he had kicked away the can after stepping on it. All the same, this close to an important race, it needed checking. With his back supported by a house wall, he felt tentatively at his foot. He looked back across the road to see if the noise had any reason behind it, and another tap lifted his eyes to see a girl's face framed in a small, square upstairs window. The girl looked to be about his age, and he thought she would normally have been pretty, with dark hair cascading around her shoulders and deep, thoughtful blue eyes, but the pallor of her face at the moment suggested she was very tired, or very afraid, or both. She was mouthing words at him and glancing anxiously behind her every few seconds.

He forgot his foot; clearly, she had little time and wanted to use it. He held up his hands in a 'stop' gesture, then pointed to his lips and beckoned her to start mouthing her words. She twitched impatiently, perhaps thinking it was some kissing motion, so he pointed at his lips again and then at his ear to try and impress on her that he could lip read. After a few seconds, she caught on – she was obviously quick on the uptake, whatever else was happening – and this time, he could follow successfully each slowly enunciated word. Her words were very disturbing, and anxiously, he mouthed them back to her, needing to be sure. She nodded and smiled quite suddenly, a smile so warm-hearted and spontaneous that a moment's shyness came over him and he bowed his head.

When he raised it, a very different face had replaced the girl's; a powerful, bull-necked man, his chin dark with stubble, his eyes hard with a glinting cruelty. He stared angrily down, then Rob saw the face disappear and could hear, even at the distance he was, a large figure noisily descending the stairs at pace. He moved rapidly away, not looking back even as he heard someone bang loudly out of the house.

Rob was confident that he could outrun the man, as he could most people; even with a slightly bruised foot, sprinting came easily to him. But when he glanced back at a safe distance, a car was already starting to move from the house.

Within two minutes, Rob made it to the beach and found a rock large enough to hide him. He needed a minute to think, even if that looked to be as long as he could afford. The girl's face, terrified, pleading, had a poignant desperation which almost moved him to tears as he remembered. And he knew the shape of her words – they could not be mistaken. He had been working at lip reading and signing ever since his brother's condition became known, not long after Daniel was born.

He controlled the wild panic in his throat as he heard the car moving slowly down the road behind the promenade at that moment as if its occupants were deciding where best to begin their search of the beach, and determined his next move.

He raced off along the promenade in the other direction, cutting through an alley to make the anonymity of the town centre before the car had time to turn round. Bearing in mind what the girl had said and the men's eagerness to catch him, there was no time to lose. The police station was on a long wide road on the other side of town; dodging and weaving across roads and pavements as fast as the terrain allowed, he entered it ten minutes after leaving the beach.

To his enormous, gasping relief, the man behind the counter was exactly who he had hoped it would be; Sergeant Pete Rawlinson, father of one of Rob's classmates and an occasional visitor to the family home. He looked at Rob and smiled.

'Rob, my son; goodness me, you are wet, aren't you?' Rawlinson began jovially, then he saw the boy's expression and the policeman returned, suspicious-eyed and waiting.

'Number 53 Harbour Road, Mr. Rawlinson – there's a girl'. Rob caught his breath and practised the rhythmic breathing he used during competition. 'She's being held there against her will, and she says she's being badly mistreated. Used as a prostitute, and sexually abused in the house'.

Rawlinson looked thoughtfully at the dripping figure before him.

'And you know this because...?'

'I can lip read, Mr. Rawlinson. You know that; for Daniel, we've always worked with lip reading as well as sign language. You must have seen us doing it'.

He saw Rawlinson still hesitating, and stepped up the urgency of his voice.

'Mr. Rawlinson, I know what she said. I could mouth the words in court if I had to, and get them verified by an expert. I know what she said'.

Rawlinson pondered, but not for much longer. He knew the house the boy was talking about; they'd been watching it for some time, and some questioning had already taken place, because of the house's proximity to where the girl had been found. Their hotel looked innocuous enough, but the big terraced places along Harbour Road were like rabbit warrens with endless nooks and crannies, basements and attics. And he knew this kid; many seventeen year olds he wouldn't have believed, with their tendency to self-dramatise and their vivid imaginations, but he'd known this kid for a long time.

'O.K., Rob, we'll go with it'. He picked up a phone. 'I'll get a car in there. And' – another grin – 'I'll get you a towel'.

By the time he gratefully managed to get under the shower at home, Rob felt worried and apprehensive; had he over-reacted to some domestic situation, and would he be faced with some irate owner demanding apologies? Much as he loathed self-pity, the storm raging about his head had started invoking dispiriting notions about being out of his depth

Back at the kitchen table with another edition of the local paper, but the atmosphere this time was very different, as Rob's father read aloud and the rest of the family listened intently.

'The dead girl's name was Iana, and her friend at the window is called Ludmila. They both came to Britain from Moldova to do an au pair sort of job, cooking and cleaning, looking after children. They and two other girls were effectively imprisoned in attic rooms in the alleged hotel. DNA comparisons between objects Iana had owned and the body discovered beneath the cliffs established her identity. Iana was being used as a prostitute and an unpaid domestic servant. Iana was a spirited girl who kept trying to get away, and police believe the people running the establishment, three men and two women, decided the girl was a threat and a nuisance and they needed to get rid of her. So they removed all evidence of identity from her and threw her off the cliff, violently enough to make sure she'd die and people would assume suicide'.

Rob's father looked across at his son and his voice raised slightly as he read on.

'The boy whose intelligent use of lip reading uncovered the criminals is below the age of eighteen and cannot be identified in view of pending court proceedings, but he is known to be a local teenager and both the girls and our community owe him heartfelt thanks for his bravery and enterprise'.

Rob saw them all watching him carefully, with the same look of pride in their eyes as Kate had had a few hours earlier, a look which felt satisfying, strengthening, like a won race.

'Is Ludmila alright?' Daniel mouthed.

'Ludmila is badly shaken, of course. But the girls have been put in contact with an agency which helps trafficked people, and their discovery and evidence will hopefully put a stop to this stuff happening in our town. We are all aware of it now'.

'And how about you, Rob, are you alright?' said Daniel.

'Yes', said Rob, unleashing an infectious grin of his own. 'Yes, brother, I'm fine'.

PLANES OF PAPER, DREAMS OF SMOKE

Josh forced his eyes away from his guitar to the crowd, a sparse affair of a couple of hundred people dotted around a theatre seating five hundred. A few were standing and spasmodically applauding, as if trying to compensate for the rather defeated atmosphere.

His twin sister Eve was giving it her all, as she always did, big, spread-armed gestures, wide blue eyes, gifting her public quick, snatched smiles as if she had a secret to share with them. She was singing their finale song, their solitary top twenty hit, now eleven and a half years old, 'The Dawn of Our Love' – 'it rose in my heart like a breaking summer day' – and, if Josh's ear could detect the fatigue in her reiteration of the song, their remaining devotees in the hall didn't seem to.

He turned his attention back to the guitar. Yes, he had played it so often that he could probably have played it in his sleep – once or twice, he had actually dreamed he was – but the last thing he wanted to inflict on Evey at the moment was a bum chord, especially when he knew what he was going to do when this performance ended.

She reached the big finish 'and tomorrow and tomorrow and tomorrow' – big arm flourish on each tomorrow – 'our love will still remain' – up note on 'main'.

Applause spattered around the hall, and the efforts at whoops and cheers by about five or six people were somehow humiliating in their sparseness.

'Goodbye', Eve shouted, 'goodbye' – he saw that she'd forgotten where they were, and to compensate – Evey thought on her feet – she told them what a marvellous audience they had been, which was a blatant lie, but Josh found himself oddly indifferent. He had a letter in his pocket, one which he hadn't dared to leave in their dressing room.

He hurried away off stage, knowing she would immediately engage with the local hangers on gathered in the wings, listening to their sycophantic lies with that head turned, strained-sweet grin of hers. He couldn't do it, but he knew why she did it, and she remained the main reason why the whole turn had lasted for so long.

Regaining the sanctuary of the dressing room, quite a generous affair compared with some of the places they'd had over the years, he got the letter out from his pocket, a single sheet of neatly typed paper. But he found he wasn't looking at the letter; he was looking at his hands, with their long slender feminine fingers, and it finally dawned on him, at the age of thirty one, just whose they resembled, almost exactly.

He was back in the Chapel, in the children's pew of seats looking down upon the stage and the altar – 'where everyone can see you, young man, including me', his father had said, followed by the slow nod which affirmed his supremacy and the advisability of obedience.

On this day, which he remembered as round about his tenth birthday, he had accidentally found himself looking directly down on his mother as she played the organ for the hymns, with such dexterity and sensitivity that even the succession of dull, plodding tunes were given an extra jolt of life. Sometimes people in the congregation would stop singing, risking the gimlet eye of his father, just to listen to her playing.

He saw her hands and fingers working across the black and white notes, dancing so deftly and unerringly, and he was mesmerised. He suddenly saw how wrong he had been to resist her offers of musical tuition. She kept saying how much it would please his father, as if she didn't realise that he regarded doing anything on that basis as a kind of treason, a betrayal of the resistance. Only weeks before that day of watching his mother's hands, he had concocted another strategy, along with a spirited friend, Joey Marten, who shared his tedium with this Chapel full of stuffy, smelly people listening for hours to boring words and repetitive music because it seemed to make them feel better about themselves.

Joey and Josh had gathered pieces of sketching paper in their pockets. They both knew well enough what the likely outcome of this scheme was going to be, but all the boys, or most of them anyway, felt some kind of resistance was long overdue to these interminable Sundays.

Down around their feet, and with wide-eyed glances and giggles from the children around them, they used their knowledge about the aero-dynamics of paper planes and replicated the designs, with broad wings and narrow tapered bodies, which had worked for them in the school yard and sometimes in the classrooms of the teachers with no control.

Crouched down so no-one below could see them, he and Joey let go the planes, two at a time – two, four, eight, ten. They looked around to see the reaction of the other kids, and the first eye he'd caught was Evey; she seemed, for some reason, to be smiling and crying at the same time. Her expression said that, even if he didn't care about what she thought, he could at least look out for himself.

The last one he launched released so well that he simply couldn't resist putting his head up over the rail to watch it. He found himself looking straight into his father's reddening face at the pulpit below, though even so, his father didn't stop singing in that great loud boom of his, accurately if more tunefully inherited by Evey. His plane did a series of spectacular swoops and dives – three, four, even five – and a subversive spot of clapping broke out in the children's pew and even here and there elsewhere. Then the plane landed right on the pulpit of the Reverend William Ryton himself, to be snatched up and pocketed by the Reverend in one swift, furious movement.

In his bedroom that same afternoon – he and Evey, even in babyhood, had never been allowed to share a bedroom – he had listened to Father, still using his sermon voice, thunder on about the sanctity of the Chapel and some other things, meaningless to him as usual, and he secretly wished his father would just get on with it, even though he knew how badly it would hurt. He remembered gazing up at the big cross above his bedhead even as his father was dropping his trousers and pants, thereby casually exposing the very same disgusting nakedness which his father always insisted that he should never reveal in any circumstances except the privacy of a locked bathroom, and even then – a really odd glance which he didn't get at all – for 'cleanliness only'.

He had already had several thrashings from Father – always 'richly deserved', apparently – but this one was vicious, with the maximum pain big flat slipper, and it went on and on until his laboriously acquired reserves of toughness expired completely and he yelled and wept like a baby.

After his father eventually stopped, stormed off and locked the door, he could hear Evey crying next door as if her heart would break. He took his lower clothes off altogether and strolled around the room letting his bottom cool down; it had become a familiar process by then. He slid out the small piece just above skirting they used to communicate.

'It's O.K., Evey. I'm O.K. It hurts, but it soon goes away'. He hoped she couldn't hear the tears still in his voice.

'It was the best plane ever, Josh', she whispered. 'One day, when we leave here, we'll fly like that, you and I, and everyone will be watching'.

Even then, she'd had the idea that the two of them would make music together. He didn't have his father's power of voice like she had, but he had his mother's ear for music, and his singing voice was good enough for the Chapel choir, which he wasn't all that happy about, but it gave him some leeway with his father. After watching Mother's hands playing, he'd asked her to teach him, and she'd chosen a guitar for him, much more portable than huge keyboards. Mother was gentle and patient most of the time; when she wasn't, and the dark eyes flashed in his direction as the mouth tightened, he saw how she had managed to keep the Reverend under control. His father knew to shut up his thundering when she had something she wanted to say and said it.

'Concentrate, Joshua, please; that isn't a difficult chord really, is it?'

She could snap him into obedience easily, just with that change of eyes; she was always telling him 'you have my family's eyes, Joshua' and when he'd worked out what she meant, it felt like his own eyes staring back at him telling him to concentrate and behave. And she could say 'stupid boy' just like the Captain in Dad's Army; that would always make him laugh, meaning she laughed, and everything was suddenly O.K.

In the dressing room, he did what he always did first, putting the guitar carefully to bed in its box like a pet in its basket – the instrument was an old friend.

He re-read the letter, a neat and legalisitic document from the agent of a group run mostly by Douglas Weston, Doogie, who had phoned Josh to ask about where things were with the Ryton Twins, because the lead guitarist of their outfit had emigrated to New Zealand for family reasons and they were in the middle of a number of recording, backing and touring commitments. Josh had asked them to put the offer in writing. The Ryton Twins had toured with the band and Josh had played on a couple of their albums. They were a dedicated R and B outfit who had had a solid following for years and were respected for their music. He thought the Ryton Twins had gone as far as they were going to go, but that didn't mean Eve would agree with him.

He could hear her making a regal progress down the corridor, stopping every few feet to react or comment – 'oh, no, I never get sick of singing 'Dawn', it has done so well for us'; 'you're very kind, but I'm not in that league, I don't think'. He put the letter hastily back in his trousers, stripped off and headed into the shower. When dressing rooms had showers, and nowadays most the ones they used did, he went straight into them after sticky gigs under hot lights. Separate dressing rooms had never been on in the early days, and they had both got used to their nakedness, disgusting or otherwise, long ago.

He heard her come in and shut the door firmly behind her. She sighed and swore quietly under her breath.

'That guy – what's his name, Reynolds, the old lech – was out there again. God, it's like being stalked. What is it now, ten years, since he's been following us around –'

She quietened, and he knew that quiet. When he came out, she was still sitting there, just gazing at the floor, and he knew she already knew. While he dried and dressed, the silence remained oppressive, as if a wall had raised between them.

'Do you remember', she said, as if resuming an earlier conversation, 'when Cath and I put together that dry ice thing, when things were really moving for us? 'Dawn' had just entered the top forty and was tipped to go on and up, and you and I were supposed to emerge as if out of the smoke, Hammersmith Odeon, no less. Big build up. 'No folks, you're not dreaming, you're not having a vision, right here and now, your dreams have come true, it's the fabulous, the one and only, RYTON TWINS!'

'Yes, I remember', he said. 'I damn near choked to death in rehearsal'.

He smiled at her, but she didn't return the smile.

'Yes, you thought it was hilarious, didn't you? When we did the rehearsal, when the legendary Ryton Twins took up their places on stage, you almost pissed yourself, didn't you? I knew then it was more my dream than yours, big time stardom, glitz and bling –'

'Evey, it was only a stunt, for God's sake –'

'Oh, yes, but I remember what you said. When you'd stopped laughing, that is. 'This is all showbizzy crap. We're about music. O.K., it might be middle of the road, but it's still music. I'm a musician, not a clown. I can't play a guitar properly in a room on fire'. One of the longest speeches I ever heard from you on tour, Josh –'

'Look, Evey –' he started, and his guts were wrenching again, as they now did too often.

She started to take off her clothes.

''I'm a musician, not a clown'. That's what you've always thought to yourself really, isn't it? All this time, clowning around. And that's where you're going, isn't it? A bloody musician'.

Her eyes flashed anger at him.

'I've seen you putting that paper in your pocket like it was a bloody hand grenade at least three times now. Big secret, Josh, eh? When have we ever had big secrets?'

She stormed past him into the shower.

'O.K, Eve, we need to talk –'

'Tell me at the hotel!' she shouted back. 'I'll be able to cope by then!'

He reached the hotel gratefully and anonymously; he had had enough of people, after gigs, for a while at least. The Ryton Twins still had enough clout to allow themselves a room each, even if the hotel was no Ritz. He had a balcony, and he stepped out into the night air, cool but not bitingly so, looking towards the fields and a nearby village; the view was familiar enough, they had played this town several times before. In any case, it was not far from his school, his Great Escape, as he thought of it. By the age of eleven, he had changed his tactics with the Reverend and realised how to enlist the clever support of his mother. He was already showing promise in both music and sport, his disgusting nakedness apparently not forbidding him from joining the local swimming club – he heard his mother's voice once again – 'cleanliness, athleticism, are all next to godliness, William – ' even if there was apparently no question of Evey doing likewise. He was sent to a school with a reputation for training clergymen. He persuaded his boyish mind to connive at the deception, even with his mother, that he aimed to train for the priesthood when, from the very first day, he had no intention of entering any profession with his father in it.

He expected to hate the place; he thought being away from the Reverend would be the only thing it had going for it, and expected further beatings, if at least clothed. But it turned out radically better than he'd expected. His teachers were able and talented, and when it was emphatically confirmed by a sympathetic housemaster that his father's punishment methods had been illegal in education for some time, a more positive attitude grew in him. He also knew instinctively that the housemaster in question had an eye to his welfare from that time onwards. Between eleven and sixteen he prospered. His piety, even if largely feigned, and his progress smoothed things when he went home in the holidays.

Evey was also changing, and he wasn't sure it was for the better. She, too, made steady progress with music especially; shortly after her fifteenth birthday, she came into contact with Cath, a young teacher and charity worker who organised musical entertainments for charity gigs and school performances. Cath helped Eve compete in talent contests and local productions, and Eve notched up successes from the start, though to Josh they didn't seem to remove the persistent melancholia which came to characterise his sister.

When Evey came to meet him in the nearby town – she found the boys' school intimidating – friendly and funny as she still was, there was something subdued about her, something not right, and all his clumsy teen attempts to get to the root of it failed, as far as he was concerned. Something was happening, and it disturbed him, even in the much improved atmosphere of his schooling. He felt he had somehow deserted her.

During the summer holidays before his final A level year, everything came to a head. On an August day, Josh was in his room which now resembled a student study room. The cross he had looked at just before the worst of his father's thrashings had been put away in a drawer. The Reverend had protested, of course, but Josh was seventeen and the fiction of training for the priesthood was no longer necessary. He had his father's family's height and was already six foot two, an inch taller than the Reverend. Josh was a school prefect, was part of a school 'group' which played gigs in the school and its local area, and his sport and swimming had given him the physique to match his height.

He was wrestling with his incomplete notes on music history and theory units when he became aware of raised voices downstairs. He tried to ignore them – events downstairs were generally no business of his – but his father's mounting boom against a couple of patient female voices convinced him that this was a family matter which might involve him. Sighing, he shelved the notes and went downstairs.

In the front lounge, ornately furnished and maintained by his mother, a group of four people were assembled. His father was leaning forward in the big Chesterfield armchair to the left of the artificial fire, his face suffused with anger. His mother was in her customary less spectacular armchair opposite him, and on the sofa sat Eve, next to a young woman with short, neat hair who he would normally think of as quite pretty, if austerely so, but at the moment the pallor of her skin spoke of nervousness and even fear.

Josh was in a t-shirt, shorts and sandals, standard wear for a warm day, in his book. His father, in his usual all-black with a white clerical collar, turned to look at him as he came in and his brow blackened. At one time, this would have cowed him from the start, but those days were gone and he knew it, even if his father didn't.

'For pity's sake, boy, will you dress yourself suitably before coming into the best room in the house?' said William Ryton.

'My dress is suitable enough for a warm August day, I think, Father. What seems to be the problem here?'

Cath took courage from this defiance. She had never met Josh before, and the sudden appearance of another gigantic man had almost caused her to bolt from the room, self-contemptuous as it would have made her. Of course, she had heard a lot about Josh, and the fact that he did have the independent turn of mind his sister described gave her the encouragement she needed. As the Reverend tutted loudly and turned away, Cath decided to address Josh. Eve was sitting still, seemingly almost frozen, her eyes firmly on the ground.

'Nice to meet you at last, Josh. I'm here to speak for your sister, concerning aspects of her relationship with her father with she is personally too intimidated to do much about, aspects which, I have to say, do to me amount to a kind of abuse'.

The Reverend was on his feet, alongside his son, and Cath physically flinched away.

'How dare you come into this house and presume to talk of things of absolutely no concern to you? Get out before I throw you out, woman!'

Josh made his voice firm and clear, even if it had a tone of lightness.

'Come now, sir, that is hardly gallant. This lady and Eve have known each other for some time, I know, and I think we should at least hear what she has to say'.

'Don't tell me what to do, boy. It's the Devil's work, when sons rebel against fathers –' his father said, but the Reverend had just got the full voice of his wife's dark eyes.

Josh took his opportunity; he, too, could read those eyes.

'I feel it is for the lady of the house to decide, Father, is it not? This is, after all, her house. Is it your wish that we hear what the lady has to say, Mother?'

Mary Ryton wrestled with herself, but only briefly. Her beliefs in relation to marriage imposed on her a duty of obedience towards her husband, but her instinct told her that something was very wrong here.

'Yes, Josh, thank you, I think it is. Something has clearly upset Eve very much, and I want to know what it is. We can only deal with it, William, when we know what it is'.

The Reverend was on his feet again, and Josh's heartbeat accelerated at the thought of a physical confrontation, even as he surprised himself by seriously considering it as a possibility. But it seemed his father was intent on strategic withdrawal.

'I never thought the day would come when I would be openly defied in my own house. I have duties to attend to at the Chapel, and I shall do so now, and I will pray that the natural order of things might re-assert itself as soon as possible'.

He stormed out. Cath let out a big sigh; Josh immediately sat down in his father's chair. The Reverend shot him a final furious look before leaving the room.

Cath seized her moment.

'For some years now, I gather, Eve has been subjected to what her father has described as 'submissions and penances', to apparently 'learn obedience', 'understand the obscenity of lust' and other such ideas. They have taken both physical and, not infrequently, sexual forms. Until now, Eve has told no-one because she lacks the appropriate vocabulary, nor did she understand what the things being done to her represented. She felt they were clearly her father's will and consequently it was her duty to obey'.

And, as everyone froze to immobility, Cath described in explicit language the nature of the 'submissions and penances'. Josh's anger mounted in him rapidly, and both he and his mother knew the truth of what was being said simply by looking at Eve, now in tears.

Now, sitting in his hotel room after what was probably the last gig the Ryton Twins would ever do, Josh remembered the developments which followed quickly on that terrible day like dominoes falling; his father's blustering denials and eventual attempted justification, his mother's cold, dreadful anger, Eve retreating to a girls' flat share arranged for her by Cath, his parents' divorce, uncontested by his father and at the end of his own schooling, Eve and he setting up house together with their mother. Estranged, his father emigrated after a year, which Josh strongly suspected as being a cover-up arranged by the Church.

Looking back over the fourteen years now between him and that day, Josh sometimes suspected that it might have been the evil done to his sister that made him devote his musical abilities to the Ryton Twins dream. He also felt a clinging sense of guilt when he reflected that his departure for school seemed to have turned his father's strange self-hating viciousness towards his children on to Eve, with an added sexual dimension, though it dawned on him eventually that being stripped for punishment had a sexual intention of itself. He also found out, some years after leaving school, that his housemaster had spoken privately to the Reverend and made clear the school's view, reinforced by the housemaster quoting some very senior clerical connections. His final beating from his father, watered down by comparison, happened when he was twelve, and then all physical punishment stopped; now he thought he knew why. And who had become the new target.

But he knew there was more to the Ryton Twins than that. Eve was good, very good; tutored by Cath, she had the voice, the guts and the looks to perform, and Josh was able to find a lyric writer from his old school band to co-write some of the songs – 'The Dawn of Our Love', dedicated to a girl Josh's friend was seeing at the time, took half an hour in a theatre dressing room after an early gig. For a while, the Ryton Twins had threatened to hit the really big time – the 'right-on twins', one music paper had called them, and it stuck for some time. But the follow up to 'Dawn' didn't drag itself above number 42, and two years later, they were a minor band backing other people. And yes, the Hammersmith Odeon clouds of smoke happened at about the crossroads; perhaps his unwillingness to walk into Evey's dreams of smoke did signify the end.

He had made sacrifices along the way; he had submitted, under protest, to wearing some of Cath's outfits, a few of which left almost his entire torso bare. When, to Eve's great amusement, knickers started being thrown at him on stage and photos of him in Cath's outfits started appearing in fan mags, he realised it wasn't just his music that he was contributing. Eve knew well enough about his changeable sex life, the endless stream of affairs large and small, ranging from post-performance one-offs to a few weeks, rarely but occasionally, months. All he knew about her love life was the suitors being politely but firmly rejected, one after the other, and he now thought a make-up girl called Melanie, who had toured with them for years, had become more than a make-up girl to Eve. Josh didn't see it as his business. Evey was entitled to work that out as she wanted, perhaps even more so after what had been done to her. He and Evey were now thirty one; after five albums, all of which sold reasonably well, especially the first two, one big hit and several minor ones, they were both comfortably off. Josh had also substantially benefited from song-writing, and not just for the Ryton Twins. He could afford to do what he liked. But if it meant deserting Eve, he wasn't sure he did like.

He heard a knock on his door, and he answered it; of course, it was Eve, and with her was a room service guy with a bottle of champagne in an ice bucket and two glasses.

'Are you on for a glass or two, Josh?' she said, with just a touch of waver in her voice.

'Yes. Sure. I'm out on the balcony, enjoying the night air. If it's not too cold for you'.

'It won't be'.

She and the room service guy processed across to the balcony and the guy left, not before she'd given him a fiver; she was good like that. They sat either side of the table and he smiled across at her as he opened the bottle.

'Pretty neat, Evey. I was expecting a row'.

'I was heading for one', she said. 'Then I spoke to people'.

'People including Melanie?'

She looked sharply across at him, then her face relaxed.

'Of course. I might have known you'd have worked that one out by now. Melanie and I have been what I suppose you'd call an item for a while'.

He got up, leaned over the table and kissed her lightly on the cheek.

'I'm happy for you, Evey'.

'Oh, Josh', she said, and their embrace confirmed what was in both their minds.

'So is the champagne for that, or is it to sign off the Ryton Twins?' Josh said.

'A bit of both, I suppose', Eve said. 'Melanie would like me to go off with her on a long holiday, Paris, Madrid, Rome, wherever, and work out what we do next. I've been resisting so far, because I didn't want to break up the Twins; I suppose I mis-read you, and then I was annoyed with myself for being so stupid. You're my twin brother, for heaven's sake; I ought to be able to read you like a book'.

'Well, if that's how it's supposed to be the other way round, it's never worked for me. You're the same enigma as you've always been. But usually in a good way'.

She put her hand on his arm. He heard her again, weeping for him in the room next door.

'But what will you do, Josh? I mean, not about music, or money; you have no problems with either of them. I mean someone. Or have the stage knickers and the kind of letters you get sent – oh, yes, I've seen some of them, I could hardly fail to – led you to think there's only one thing women are good for?'

His hand joined hers; he remembered watching her watching their father as he preached, her eyes alight with pride, and he had to stop himself from crying out.

'Evey, if either of us have cause to be disgusted with the opposite sex, I'd say your cause was better than mine. I just don't need a permanent partner yet; I'm sort of married to the music, if that's not too corny. But I dare say I will, in time, and you'll be the first to know'.

'O.K., Josh'. Their hands separated as they picked up their glasses.

'Here's to the Ryton Twins, brother. It was a blast'.

'It sure was, Evey. Cheers'.

JENNIFER'S ROOM

For the last time, Jennifer locked the door and, even now, her accusing inner voice nagged the absurdity of it at her, locking a door in an empty house. On previous occasions, she would retaliate with assertion; she was a middle-aged woman on her own, and any measures she thought necessary for her safety were entirely legitimate. This time was simply about the need to say goodbye to her erstwhile sanctuary, as privately as possible.

In her teens, the room had been an escape and refuge in so many ways, including surroundings of contemporary simplicity rather different from the ornate, chintzy taste desert of the rest of the house, so resolutely championed by her mother.

'Yes, Jennifer, it may be fussy and sentimental in your view, but when you have lived in some of the places I've lived in, fussy and sentimental is nice – colourful, warm'.

Her mother had lived in a permanent state of moral indignation about something or other, up to and including Jennifer's own rigorous cancer monitoring regime. Jennifer's grandmother had died of an ailment described in a fatuous euphemism of the time as 'a spreading chest-based infection', but Jennifer read it as breast cancer, and had started having herself checked even before she left home. The fact that her mother subsequently paid such a terrible price for studiously ignoring the risk gave Jennifer no pleasure whatever. It was one more bewildering conundrum in a life liberally sprinkled with them.

And in those teen days, the options of her own domain would open up to her with gratifying immediacy as soon as the door was closed and locked. She spent ludicrously indulgent amounts of time lolling about on her squarely-built, plain blue sofa reading writers who wrote about 'people like her', a phrase which had taken her all of her youth to finally acknowledge and which was, apparently, her mother's most serious 'apprehension' about her, according to her father, though never once in her lifetime did her mother say as much. She could keep up her spasmodic social media contacts, though actually meeting them face to face was still a leap too far. She could check to see her books – 'do you really **need** so many books, Jennifer?' – her mother would say, as if they were toilet paper – remained in accessible order, and her clothes likewise.

Now she told herself she was enjoying the pleasant anticipation of knowing that very soon workmen would be tramping through the house removing the flowery wallpaper and patterned carpets once and for all in order to make the house saleable. She intended to supervise a lot of the work herself, and she thought she would enjoy the men's company.

Her denials of her mother's dark hints about man-hating as a result of Jennifer's resolute lack of 'relationships' – 'I know they can be gross and horrid, Jennifer, but we do have to find a way of sharing the planet with them' – had always been perfectly genuine. She found men simpler than women, and usually better company, and the fact that she was not sexually attracted to them was release rather than restriction. Sometimes, they seemed to sense it; in her teaching days, the boys rarely played her up or practised their primitive flirting techniques with her, and would even sometimes take her part against the more suspicious, subtle girls, especially the older ones, only too ready to put interpretations on teachers' lack of opposite sex partners.

But the greatest plus for her room in her recent adult stay had become the surrounding silence. The lock started in her teens as one of her earliest rebellions against her mother, a direct consequence of her mother's cavalier attitudes to knocking – 'you haven't got anything I haven't seen, dear' – and later on, it had grieved her to have to use it against her father, but when his illness was developing, any noise from outside the room meant he was once again randomly up and about. On several occasions, she had found him in the garden in his dressing gown – twice, urinating up against the side of the shed – and there had been various degrees of undress to deal with. An alarming clunk had once forced out of her room to find him sitting in his pants with his back against the side of the bath; she concluded that he must have actually fallen asleep while standing to use the toilet.

Every occasion was a defeat, the inner nagger demanding why she hadn't thought of this contingency, and the eventual night locking of both front and back doors, denying him access to the keys, felt like a humiliation for both of them. The subsequent 'situation update' – his term – with her brother Simon had been sticky after that.

'I know it's not easy, Jen' – Simon was the only person in the world who had ever called her Jen rather than Jennifer, and that of itself gave her a lot of time for him – 'but can we actually lock him in? Is that permissible? Is it legal, for that matter?'

For once, her temper had got the better of her.

'Simon, he's been in the garden several times, once half naked. On two occasions, I only just got to the gate before he'd walked off into the street. He still recognises my voice, just about; before long, he won't, and then we will find ourselves scouring the town or calling the police. We've agreed that we want to keep him out of an institution for as long as we can, and I appreciate you are mainly funding the day time care workers, but when I'm on my own, I have to do what I have to do'.

He looked shame-faced, as he had been as a child when confronted with some minor dereliction of duty. Her mother ran the two of them like a well-practised domestic workforce, with rotas for washing up, bed-making, room cleaning, etc. and enforced homework periods. The regime was supposedly backed up by paternal physical discipline; 'I will call on your father if it becomes absolutely necessary, be sure of it', though they both knew their father had limits beyond which he would not be pushed, and 'groundings' or pocket money fines had always been the worst fates on offer, in spite of Mother's apocalyptic mutterings.

The adult Simon's anguish on his father's behalf had brought her back to the house she had been so keen to leave when a university place came along. In her late thirties, she was finding teaching exhausting and repetitive, the innovative delights of the early years fading. She remained without a 'significant other'. Having finally come to terms with 'people like her', she wanted a relationship, especially now her mother was no longer around to have to explain things to, but she hadn't the nerve or yet the confidence to go beyond social media into the real world of meetings and relationships.

She moved back into the family house, intending a 'breather'; being good with money, she could afford a transition time, and she knew that, two years after his wife's death, her father was finding it increasingly difficult to cope. The plan was to look after him while taking a break from work to make her mind up about whether she should seek another full-time job, or consider part-time or supply teaching, or attempt entry into further education.

Shortly after her return, Simon had summoned a 'family conference', the family consisting of Jennifer, Simon and Simon's wife Helen, who was up and down most of the time attending to their two grumpy pre-teen boys. Simon eventually took her into his office, where even Helen was wary of bursting in. Simon, like herself, was a more assertive personality than his father, and she felt a fellowship with the solidity of his character.

'Look, Jen, I am not, repeat not, trying to say you are any more responsible for looking after Dad than I am; there is no stereotyping stuff going on her. He clearly is slipping into illness; Mum so organised his life that he's like a rudderless ship without her anyway. I can't move back into the house; I've got a family to look after. Which is not to assume that you should take on anything you don't feel you can handle. Our choices are simple; you either move back in, or we finance care workers more or less round the clock, or –'

'Or we put him in a home'.

Negotiations continued, though she had a growing sense that moving back into the house without, yes, in all honesty without, the problems of coping with her mother, might be an opportunity to re-ground herself and eventually, a compromise was reached. It did involve the household being partly financially supported by Simon, which could have been a sticking point, but Simon was an architect and his wife a designer, and she knew they were very comfortably off. Nevertheless, she made her position very clear.

'I will carry on for as long as I think it feasible, Simon, on condition that we do have some care worker support – I will contribute to that as well as I can. But if the doctors are right and his condition is both mentally and physically degenerative, then there will come a point where it will no longer be feasible, and it will have to be care in an institution'.

It had been feasible for almost four and a half years, largely because she had made it so. Her father had always been a gentle, humorous man, articulate and affectionate if in a slightly detached, guarded way. In the early stages, there had been moments when they could and did talk with a greater sympathy and honesty with each other than ever before, and though he would never say as much, it became clear to Jennifer that he had relied on his wife rather more than he'd ever actually loved her. By profession, he'd been a quantity surveyor – it was sometimes accompanying him in his trips round the building sites which had originally excited Simon's interest in architecture – and all his limited capacities for administration and timing were used up in his work. Jennifer realised that his gradual disintegration had probably started before her mother had died, and the realisation was another strand of the reappraisal of her mother's life which her sense of justice had forced upon her.

Her father's state, and the advice she gleaned from everywhere she could, brought her to appreciate from the start that the thorough professionalism she had brought to her teaching could be applied to her care regime for him, even if the context was different. She collected many of the old photographs which had been lying about the house undisturbed in cupboard drawers and filing cabinets for years, boxes of articles consigned to the attic by her ever-practical mother. She concentrated particularly on the ones from her father's past, some of them his long past, and even in his most abstracted states she could sometimes haul him back to her by using these albums, which she worked on diligently until there were several large collections she could alternate between. She bought a DVD player, and with Simon's help and sometimes his money, obtained material of old newsreels, individual years from her father's youth, old comedy programmes, old films and Simon's home movies of his family. These sessions could take up entire afternoons, and, for a while, they could finish with her father more animated and conversational than she could remember him for years.

It was ultimately a losing battle, she knew well enough, but it became her cause and she promised herself that it would go to the very last ditch. When there was nothing left but her father's blank stares, when every breakfast time became an ordeal of packets he couldn't open, food which would finish on the floor, and sudden leavings of tables, rooms and even the whole house, she knew that even the care workers' support would soon not be enough. The times when she was dealing with him on her own began to include doing things which became more and more intimate, but it was impatience rather than disgust which moved her, nudging her as it did into territory where she didn't know the ground and felt the role was becoming intrusive and even presumptuous.

In the last few weeks before she bowed to the inevitable, her decision supported by an increasingly anxious Simon, the social worker she saw changed from the dour, cynical May to the more amenable Beth, a few years younger than Jennifer herself. Beth was as efficient as she was friendly, and contributed valuably to fixing up both the institution and the financial arrangements. On the quiet, rather desolate days following her father's admittance to the care home, Beth was there from time to time to comfort, console and argue the inevitability of it all with a warmth and sympathy which Jennifer appreciated.

It was during one of Beth's visits, while they were sitting close to each other and discussing matters relating to her father's care in the home, that their eyes met with a look which even Jennifer's naivete and inexperience could not fail to understand. They realised simultaneously that their relationship was moving beyond professional issues. Suddenly, Jennifer's musings, which she usually dismissed as wishful thinking, about Beth's single status and the total absence of talk about men, lewd, indignant or otherwise, from her conversation, clicked into the reality she had always hoped for.

In her room and on her bed, with the door locked and no more questioning about it from Beth than a momentary raising of the eyebrows, Jennifer finally discovered what love-making was all about for her in one, long glorious afternoon. The first time they approached the whole business tentatively, cautiously, with Jennifer terrified of a recoil of disgust from Beth, or even more painfully, from herself, which could kill the affair stone dead in its infancy, but there were no recoils of disgust, just a mutual realisation that each stage had been successfully reached and the next one promised even more. Beth was clearly much more experienced and, she considered, much more attractive than she was, and the very obvious fact that Beth found Jennifer's nakedness not only attractive but exciting was such a liberating discovery that confidence flowed into Jennifer like some newly discovered panacea. The regular sessions at the local pool, generally fixed more to the care workers' convenience than her own, which the inner nagger had dismissed as unnecessarily austere, were gloriously vindicated in her mind.

She had her first proper orgasm at the age of thirty six, in the very room where even her shame-faced fumblings under the sheets using her imagination – she dared not buy magazines in the teeth of her mother's remorseless housework efficiency – had occurred only after the room lock had been acquired and its efficiency put to the test.

A few days later, the exercise was repeated in almost every particular, except this time the door was closed but not locked, and one week later, the door was flung wide open throughout another experience and further exploration. Afterwards, as they lay naked on the bed together, Jennifer suddenly found herself feeling something which she could only understand as a state of euphoria as she gazed, unafraid and unashamed, through her open door and into the house outside.

Of course, the inner nagger's revenge for such a drastic sequence of defeats was not long delayed, and only a few days after the open door experience, her father had a massive heart attack which killed him, at the age of 77, before an ambulance could even be summoned.

A kind of guilt returned, but it had a different quality and emphasis. She had already moved beyond guilt about her relationship with Beth and what they did together, but she no longer felt comfortable about doing it in the parental home.

'More a matter of taste than guilt, really, darling', she said, to Beth's concerned questions. 'I made my room mine, but only because the rest of the house was theirs. It has taken me long enough to leave; now I really think I should'.

Negotiations began with Simon, and both he and Helen were generous enough to insist that Beth joined in. She was touched if a little disconcerted to discover how solicitous and understanding they were, even the boys, Peter and Mark, who, it seemed, did actually quite like her, another revelation in an apparently endless sequence of them.

It was agreed that the house would be updated, dressed and put on the market, and the proceeds divided between Simon and herself. She and Beth would initially try life in Beth's beautiful but rather compact flat, but if they decided on a larger place, they would combine forces with Jennifer's share of the house and Beth's proceeds from her flat to buy a larger home. Jennifer's secret provisio to herself was that even if things didn't ultimately work out with Beth, her life in the room was as over as her isolation and self-denial.

Sooner or later, the moment had to come, and today, at last, it was here. She heard Beth's car draw up on the front drive. Her cases were already stacked in the hall, and with two cars, they would probably manage, for the moment, anyway.

She unlocked the door and gazed round the room, now stripped down enough to look abandoned and rather forlorn. The doorbell sounded. She closed the bedroom door gently behind her and moved towards the front door, without looking to the right or left.

HIGH TIDE

Boys were milling about the quadrangle, some encroaching on the central lawn area, and the noise level was growing. He was looking down the corridor, calculating how strong his prefect's reaction should be, regretting any unpleasantness while acknowledging its necessity.

Then a curtain cracked like a flag, and he woke and remembered that school had finished weeks ago and the hum was the nearby sea. The only other sounds were a morning breeze and racking coughs from his father in the adjoining bedroom, which continued even through Father's brief periods of sleep. Cambridge in less than two months now, unless he enlisted or was called up; he could wish for a less brutal adulthood initiation. Ben Foreman, eighteen years old just over one month ago, was now subject to the Military Service Act in force as of March 2nd 1916. Someone might argue, perhaps through his father's contacts, that his scientific work should exempt him; otherwise, call up or enlistment were his only options.

This cottage, isolated in a Devon cove, a holiday home for their little family since his childhood, seemed now their last chance of rallying his father's health with sea air and merciful privacy, but that cough had come to sound like demonic laughter at the fading hopes of Ben and his mother.

Ben left his bed and went to the window. He determined on a morning swim – at 7.30 on a summer morning, the water would be initially cool enough to catch the breath, but soon adjusted to. He needed only a towel; there was no-one but his parents to see him. He was tall, and at eighteen, proportionately man-shaped after adolescent vagaries of limbs seeming to follow separate timetables. With calm brown eyes and aquiline good looks, high cheek-boned and long nosed, Ben knew when eyes were resting on him by the school swimming lake, and he'd had a few guilty adventures amongst the trees. But that was then.

He aimed to go straight to the sea, but his eyes were unable to pass his father's paper from yesterday still on the kitchen table. Wednesday July 19th 1916, and the reports full of the dreadful confrontations taking place on the Somme at Delville Wood and Pozieres, in which the Allied armies were apparently storming on to inevitable victory with few losses of their own, although they had already been doing so for nearly three weeks and reports from soldiers on leave filtered through a different story of a vicious and hellish encounter slowly becoming the bloodiest battle ever fought in the history of mankind.

It took several minutes of restless paper-shuffling before the boy still inside him clamoured and he ran out of the cottage and straight down to the sea, throwing the towel down just before he entered the water. As he'd anticipated, only a few minutes' movement were necessary to turn the first eye-watering chill into the comfort of a bath.

As an easy, well-practised swimmer, his mind could work on other matters while he swam. Father had tried to find solutions.

'You're a scientist, Ben. You can contribute in that way just as usefully as taking part in the actual combat'.

His father was usually a solid, reassuring man, even in illness. But now Ben thought he could see an evasion about the eyes, occasionally flickering away or glancing downwards.

'I'm a scientist whose main concern is plants and creatures, Father. It's difficult to see how that can make any meaningful contribution to a war'.

'We may well have to fight in many different places. You've always said to me that natural history can provide information about terrain, climate, water depths, land travel. Such knowledge will be invaluable to planning of invasions and military actions abroad. When, of course, you graduate – that must, Ben, be your priority'.

Ben had nodded, as dutiful sons did, producing a thin smile in the appeased way of fathers properly obeyed. But they both knew the subject was far from closed.

Now, even the ease and freedom of the water could not supersede the troubles of his mind. He had swum strongly, and when he stopped and turned to look back on the coast, he saw a panorama of serenely beautiful Devon coast next to the pure blue sea and his eyes suddenly, embarrassingly, flooded with tears. He controlled himself, submerging and rising again until only legitimate moisture remained on his face, and set off back towards the coast.

He regained the shore and sat down on the towel, reluctant either to confront the decision he had to make or to go back too quickly to the remorseless coughing and sober defeat of the cottage. A few explorations had already revealed creatures living especially in the little rock pools between the boulders at the bottom of the cliff. He knew what they were and none of them was unusual in this part of the world, but the brilliant light of the Devon morning tempted him to spend time watching.

Moving across the rocks, his big feet clutching on to the cool, solid surfaces, he found a new and larger rock pool. So much happening; the shore crabs were scampering between pools when they weren't feeding on anything which looked even vaguely edible. The limpets looking firmly fixed to their surfaces, though in fact, they were essentially snails and they moved around coherently, leaving trails to allow them to find their way back; some of them lived in their pool universe for twenty years. Beadlet anemones sat out of the water like little red blobs of jelly, but once immersed, would let loose over two hundred tentacles to pick up fish and prawns for feeding. He saw a cushion starfish, aptly named with their satin sheen, tiny things which could rest easily on a single finger. So outrageously un-human, beginning life male and changing to female at about the age of four, and with five arms, each of which, if lost, would simply grow back. He picked two of them up, very carefully, and placed them on his hand for closer inspection.

The war question, when it arrived, changed his mood in a moment. Were people who enjoyed wandering naked along shores looking at tiny marine creatures and found appalling the thought of anyone damaging their living places capable of fighting wars? He returned the starfish to their pool and sat dejectedly on the rock, his head sinking into his hands. He either had to have the courage to fight or the courage to refuse to; the attitudes of boys and masters at school made the stories of what was being done to the 'conchies' not difficult to believe. Between the devil and the deep blue sea, an image very appropriate in this place.

Gazing out to sea for distraction, he saw a distant fishing boat setting out. The boat was unthreatening and normal, but it took no great effort of imagination to visualise larger, more hostile boats filling the horizon. Hard as it was to envisage himself violating the harmless and innocent, it would be equally impossible for him to sit passively by while others were. If only savagery could defeat savagery, so be it. It was about means and ends, intentions and destinations. So the ultimate contradiction, the final irony, seemed to form itself into a need to dehumanise to protect the right to be human.

The morning felt soiled, the pleasure of the swim distant and trivial. He moved to the shore and picked up the towel. He had taken the decision which needed taking. But nothing could persuade him to take any pleasure from it or the need for it.

He stepped back into the kitchen, throwing the towel on to a nearby chair, and stared from the front window at the Devon cove, wanting to register every detail; everything important to him, he thought, would now need to be remembered. Only minutes later did he hear a movement behind him and turned to see his mother sitting at the table watching him, wrapped in nightdress and dressing gown. She looked even more tired than usual, all the humour in the quizzical green eyes misted over and the lines to the side of them even deeper. He grabbed for the towel.

'Oh, don't worry, Ben, please. You always have swum naked here; I don't see anything needs to change. In any case, I'm proud of having brought something so beautiful into being. Framed against the morning light, you make an exquisite picture, probably beyond my powers now to reproduce faithfully, but the image pleases me greatly'.

'You haven't painted at all since we got here', he said, sitting next to her and laying the towel across himself for the sake of close quarter decency.

'No, I know. Your father keeps saying that I should, but I find it difficult to leave him now.

We don't have much time left, Ben'.

This was the first time she had spoken so fatalistically, and his head went down. But he had to talk, and there never would be anything like a good time.

'I've made the decision I had to make, Mother. I'm going to have to join up before they call me up. There isn't really a choice. There never was'.

He got up; he couldn't face an argument.

'I must dress; giving myself a chill will do no-one any good'.

He walked away. Ellen again turned her exhausted mind to the practicalities. There were still strategies available to retrieve at least part of the situation. John knew generals, war ministry bureaucrats, army administrators. The boy could serve at a divisional headquarters, or be attached to science groups working on government projects. White feathers and whispers, perhaps, but she would not, could not, give Ben up without a fight for the sake of some convoluted nonsense between interbred European monarchies. Nepotism, favouritism, whatever the labels put on it, dirty fights needed dirty tactics.

She walked back to their bedroom and saw that John had woken up. The thin, pinched features were a gross caricature of his former friendly good looks, with eye bags almost more pronounced than the eyes themselves. But harassed as they were, their intelligence and humanity had not entirely gone yet.

'Ben's been swimming, John. I'm jealous. I caught him standing naked, framed in the kitchen window, still and perfect like a Michelangelo statue'.

The cough replied. She sat beside the bed.

'I heard something about a decision', he said.

'He's going to join up'. There could be no prevarications between them, she thought. They were the luxuries of time.

His head sank back on to the pillow and his eyes closed as if his back had been stabbed.

'I'll write to people, find him a commission with one of the research groups, perhaps. I know several relevant possibilities relating to invasion possibilities in vulnerable parts of Europe'. '.

She pulled the curtains back and a stream of sunlight fell across the bed, throwing into daylight his body's pitiful skinniness. She gulped briefly, once, and hurried into speech.

'I'm not sure he'd agree. He's grown up, John. That damn school, I suppose, they beat, frighten and extort boyhood out of them. We will have to come to terms'.

He coughed again, this time unstoppably. She helped him to some water. Eventually, he quietened and lay back.

'We'll talk to him later. Properly. Work out details'.

'I'm going to prepare some food, John. You must try to eat something'.

She clicked the door behind her. From the kitchen window, she saw a dressed Ben step out of the door and walk slowly across to the rock pool. The tide was well in, the rock pools fewer and larger. She saw him pause at the side of one and gaze down, entirely absorbed. How beautifully the damn uniform would sit on him, she thought. She shuddered and turned away.

HOUR OF THE WOLF

Green figures, piercing in the gloom, say 02.52. The house is silent but for the sea. Even on becalmed nights like this, it murmurs and grumbles in the near distance, and the effect is pacifying or menacing, depending on the state of mind of the listener.

For me, it is intimidating now. I am thirty-eight, and I have been living here since the age of four. At no time has silence ever been a feature of this house. Even at this time, the hour of the wolf, associated more than any other with death and birth, I could easily be woken up by the dull thud of my father's footsteps in his studio, part of which was – still is – directly above my head. Were I to hear them now, seven months after his death, I suppose such sounds ought to terrify me, but I doubt they would; they represented a kind of normality, or as near to normality as anything associated with my father could be.

I glance across at the door. For some weeks after his death, I deliberately left it open, so I could see right across the landing and the big room beyond, living room and social space, linking onto a balcony the size of a large patio with its views over the nearby cliffs and the English channel beyond. Now this is all mine, was my first superficial line of post-funeral thought; now I can go anywhere in it without fear of sudden situations putting me completely out of my depth, usually to do with being irretrievably manacled together with the two powerful and conflicting spirits who inhabited the place through my childhood and most of my adolescence.

But it didn't take much more than a month before different feelings began to surface. Deprived of the people who so fully occupied it, the place is more of a liability, a pink elephant, than a worthwhile new possession. Probably in less than sixty years now, the garden and then the house will start to slide down into the water and never be seen again; in my thirty four years here, part of what I suppose should be called the garden has simply slithered away. Here, now, in these deadly silent small hours, it feels as if my life has itself slowly eroded, and I remain here like a relic after all the place's importance and activity has departed. My sense of new possession warped itself into deprivation.

So the door is now closed, and I retreat to my own space as I have so often done before, even though all the rest of it is now mine as well.

I already know that I have no chance of further sleep. Dawn is the best part of two hours away, and I will soon tire of lying here. He, my dad, Will, never William, Bill or Billy, he is largely responsible for the erratic hours I keep, now well into adulthood. It could be only just after the crack of dawn that my door would suddenly be flung open, and there he would be, the sweat and wood smoke smell of him already in the room. In the summer, it would be unlikely that he would be wearing anything but old shorts and sandals without socks.

'Lynda? Lyn?' His voice would start gently, regardless of having already woken me up with the flinging of the door. 'Great morning for a forage, girl. Up for it?'

I got into the habit of sleeping in something which would only need jeans put on over it and I would follow him out, usually without protest or complaint. He seemed to hold me like a magnet, and I could no more defy his wishes that I could define my own with any certainty.

The forage would be for driftwood, sea shells, bits of tourist debris, bird feathers, occasionally magazines or even books. On several occasions, we found dead animals who had managed to drown themselves by swimming too far and then not finding a suitable bit of coast to enable them to get back to dry land. Sometimes, disturbingly, items of clothing; sometimes, inexplicable machine parts; sometimes contraceptives or needles. Almost all of the Jurassic coast stretched away to the east, dotted with tourist resorts and coastal villages, and its debris could find itself washed up in the shallow bay beyond our garden.

We could spend entire mornings hunting for his latest random miscellany, and he could become genuinely excited at what had been collected. What made him, for me, the world's greatest conjuror and the spirit shining over my life like a life-giving sun was what he could then do with the stuff. Sometimes it would be paintings, gruesomely disturbing still lives suggestive of death or chaos, or arresting compositions with colour and shape combinations to take the breath away. Sometimes they would be sculptures; one which looked for all the world as if a twisted animal-like alien had died and been washed up on the beach, one which combined the discarded tourist stuff with dead bird feathers and struggling plants in works like accusations or indictments. And in his big rambling studio which looked like someone had done several house clearances and dumped them all over the space but which also looked out to the Channel and the world beyond, I would puppy around for him – 'try that on there, Lyn'; 'no, not next to that one, over by this one'; 'put it down and move away from it for a minute'. Sometimes I would be in them, but usually just with one hand, or one foot, or a single limb across them or next to them. About once a quarter, his agent, an old school friend of his called Julian Lewis, would come and collect what he'd done and take it off to be sold, though not before they'd got hilariously drunk together and walked the beach in animated discussions about whatever came into their heads.

At quarter past three, my patience runs out and I get up and pad through to what used to be the hub of the house's social activity and the setting for my parents' increasingly acerbic confrontations. I throw back the left side of the big curtain in front of the sliding doors which connect the room to the balcony, and look over the blackness of the bay, punctuated by little gleams of light, including a Christmas tree shaped bobbing about collection of lights which probably means a crab boat earning its living. Leaving the sliding doors closed on a chilly night, I sit beside an unobtrusive table lamp opposite the very chair where, not long after my sixteenth birthday, I gazed apprehensively across at my mother's very still figure, her shape silhouetted against the sea, her dark eyes full of a final defiance and decision. Enjoying her exclusive company was relatively rare for me, and it didn't take long to establish why this was a special occasion.

'I've come to the reluctant conclusion that we're going to have to leave him to his devices, Lynda', she said. 'I can't stand it any more; the endless cheroots and their stink, the brandy, his weird eating and sleeping habits, his futile fiddling about with trash and detritus –'

I had at last acquired the confidence to argue back.

'His futile fiddling about is making him and us quite a lot of money, Mother'. 'Mum' never did suit my mother. 'He's becoming very well known; 'staggering accomplishment and diversity', the Guardian said –'

'Don't quote the bloody Guardian at me, Lynda, like one of his insufferable worshipping students. I run a business; when we came down here, the understanding was that he would help me with it, use his own talents to set us up in the tourist business. Food is not his department, yes, but he was going to sort out the décor of the restaurant, perhaps offer art classes and beach walks – fossils, shells etc. – on the side, with a view to a hotel or arts centre eventually. Now I run the business entirely on my own and come home to this mess of a place with coastal winds howling around it and him, half-dressed if dressed at all, clomping around in that great attic which takes up half the house –'

The clomping became apparent at that moment, and she swore under her breath.

'Anyway, Lynda, you are good enough to help me at the Beach Affair occasionally, so perhaps it won't be too much of an upheaval for you to be renting somewhere nearby with me. It's quite possible that your father won't notice we've gone'.

With a deep sigh like a dutiful soldier knowing the price which would need to be paid, I said what I had to, and her eyes and mouth seemed to shrink together into one as I spoke.

'I will not be forced into this kind of choice, Mother. Yes, I'll still help you in the restaurant, and yes, I'll sometimes stay with you wherever you're staying. But I'm not leaving here permanently. Here needs me. He needs me'.

'He needs no-one', she snapped back. 'I've asked him time and time again to concentrate more on what we supposedly came here to do. He nods, he makes a few pacifying noises, and then carries on doing exactly what he's doing, with these mostly female roadies, as I call them, hanging on his every word and order'.

She controlled herself with an effort. My mother was and is a shrewd and successful businesswoman, and the only place she could be contradicted was in her own home. She stood up and strolled over to the window; it was early evening, with the beginnings of a sunset, as breathtakingly beautiful as the place could be. She stood with her back to me, perfectly erect, her arms folded tightly in front of her.

'Very well, Lynda', she said at last, almost under her breath. 'I'm not trying to make you the rope in a tug-of-war between your father and I. We have tried. I'd say I've probably tried a great deal harder than he has, but his persona as it is now has made him like an alien to me. I am marginalised in my own house. He has made a world for himself, and I don't seem to be a part of it. Fortunately, I have a world of my own, and there is likewise no part in it for him'.

She turned and I saw the slightest sign of tears in her eyes, which was as near as I have ever seen to her crying. After a few more desultory conversations between them, mostly concerning 'arrangements', she did what she called a 'preliminary packing' and left a few days later. Neither of them tried to talk me into remaining permanently with them.

I felt inadequate and ineffective; to some extent, I still do, even at this distance of time. As an only child – childbirth was something my mother had no intention of doing more than once – I knew them both intimately, and while I thought I understood most of the barriers between them, the confidence and articulacy to mediate was beyond me. How many sixteen year olds are sure enough of their judgements to tell older people why they can't live with each other?

Some of it, of course, was abundantly obvious. In his personal habits, my father was a slob; he rarely wore more than a minimum of clothing, even in bad weather; he went to bed and got up whenever he felt like it; he never got dressed up and took my mother out to eat or socialise, and he had several pals like his agent he could sometimes disappear for days on end with. Their sex life, at one time persistently and embarrassingly robust, had dried up, and while he didn't do anything in the house, or not when I was there anyway, it became all too obvious at times that some of his student admirers weren't there just for the art.

But she, on the other hand, had turned slowly into a kind of Ice Queen. Born into a large and very patriarchal family, she was terrified of professional failure and anything remotely resembling poverty. Yes, she was creative herself; the menus she developed which gave the Beach Affair a reputation way beyond a café on a beach gained her respect as a chef in her own right and led, after she'd split from my father, to several more restaurants and a kind of mini-catering empire. But she reached the point where everything had to have a purpose, and she couldn't understand my father giving himself over to what she saw as such monumental futility as the sort of art he went in for. When it started making him unfeasibly large dollops of money, it exasperated rather than gratified her; for all her hard work, people management and careful admin, she was struggling to equal what he could do just 'fiddling about'.

And I knew that, even if I could have found the words at the time, she would have scorned them – 'pretentious intellectualism' is one of the accusations she threw at my father's work – and the way I'd reasoned it would inevitably have come out sounding like that.

But it was the truth, nevertheless, that my father, ever since he'd arrived on the Jurassic Coast, had simply been absorbed by his environment, to such an extent that all the other minutiae of life were even more relegated to insignificance in him than they are in most people. His awareness, the way he saw the world, was almost entirely visual; like some creatures have senses beyond all other species, even if the rest of their senses are normal or even deficient, he saw patterns, materials, ideas which other people didn't see, and he had to do something about it. He grew up in London suburbia, even then doing his best to represent the images and people around him and use the ideas they suggested, but landing on the coast, initially as a very young man, his whole being was swallowed up by it. Anyone who has lived on, or perhaps even just visited, the Jurassic Coast would not find it impossibly difficult to understand. He could see that it made him all that he'd wanted to be, that he'd banged the prison door open and he was never about to go back in.

Thinking back to the split between them, happening at such a crucial time in my life, always tires me, sooner or later, and I wake in my chair to find it is well past four and dawn is breaking over the coast. On more than one occasion, as a child and a teenager, I have sat wordlessly beside my father watching this. For most people, it is an awesome, humbling spectacle, to be taken to memory and brought out in peaceful moments; for my father, it was fuel. It told him what he should and could be doing, like some kind of creative commandment. To be idle or disobedient would be, for him, like an excommunication.

After two years of yo-yoing between the two of them and coming to terms with the growing realisation that I had inherited neither his artistic ability nor her creative ways with food, I tore myself away to university to study English and give myself a medium independent of both of them. Graduation saw me drift into journalism, which eventually and inevitably brought me back to where I'd grown up. Now I had new ways of serving my father, and his work was my entry into arts journalism both local and national. I even managed to publish a piece about my mother's place, or more accurately now, her three places.

I move across to the doors and open up the balcony. Dawn is well advanced now, and the vast bay below me, familiar as it is, holds me in the same spell as ever. It was a morning like this which presented me with the last scene I ever saw between my mother and father, played out on the lawn leading down to the fenced cliffs. They were too far away for me to hear what was being said, but I knew their body language so intimately that I could easily fill in the conversation. For once, he was alone, working conventionally on an easel, interpreting some part of the colours and complexity of the coast which he never tired of portraying. There was a strong easterly breeze, meaning the panorama below and around him was far from static and even his own shirt was billowing to his right as he sat.

She walked across to him from his left. It seemed she had simply parked her car at the front of the house and walked round to him, never bothering herself to meet and greet me on her way. She walked as she always walked, purposefully, forcefully, but on this occasion with the slightest hesitancy that he now induced in her. Most people, seeing an established artist so seriously engrossed in his work, would have experienced a reluctance to interrupt or disturb him; even she was influenced by this, but her will and her increasingly impotent anger with him refused to allow her to stop and retreat.

She had asked him several times in the weeks leading up to this when would be convenient for her to come and remove the last of her possessions from the house. I was twenty three by this time, and already used to watching performances of all kinds; an element of improvised dramatic event communicated itself from what I was seeing.

He glanced up at her briefly, and his lips formed some kind of greeting, but in the kind of throwaway style which had come to infuriate her. He turned immediately back to his easel. Her body leaned forward to him, and the breeze fully behind her momentarily made it look as if she was going to fall in to him and knock both of them, and the easel, on to the grass, to end the whole episode in a farcical heap. Her torso arrowed itself at him; his right arm, resting by the elbow on the easel, raised and his fingers brushed slowly across his forehead, a classic sign of resented distraction. She screamed something at him and turned on her heels; he stood up and shouted at her retreating figure. I saw her stop as if stabbed in the small of the back; she turned and screamed again. He spread his arms resignedly, as if even her contempt and fury saddened him more than moved him. Then he simply sat down and resumed his painting. She spun round, as if looking for someone or something to ally with her in her exasperation. She saw me, for the first time.

She walked across the grass, like a soldier on double quick time, her feet pounding down.

'Tomorrow, Lyn!' she shouted just before she disappeared down the side of the house.

'Half past two! Do me a favour and try to arrange for him not to be here!'

As it happened, he wasn't, but I didn't claim credit and she didn't ask. Luckily enough, Julian Lewis called, and they were soon off together, to laugh, binge and conspire like clever schoolboys. My mother had one of her assistants with her, a tall, attractive if wind-blown Italian boy who was clearly in love with her even if she wasn't with him, and I thought in this, as in a number of other areas, her attacks on my father were rooted in hypocrisy. She was clearly using the young man for more than just moving belongings around; he hovered around her and obeyed her every word like some well turned out puppy.

When, after the best part of four hours, her work was finished, to her clear relief, my presence in her life was acknowledged again. As the lovely Luigi waited in the van, she turned to me and, like an afterthought, reached forward to peck me on the cheek.

'Look, Lynda, you love your father, I know, and I can hardly criticise you for that; I did myself, for longer than he deserved. But he will gobble your life up, darling, if you let him'.

'Either or both of you could gobble my life up, Mother', I said. I knew how to fight my corner by then. 'In fact, most people would say you already are doing, between you'.

The face set again, but she too knew better by now, and the snapped put down that this would once have provoked was held back.

'I'm sorry we couldn't have stayed together for you. Perhaps he is a genius; perhaps we both are, which is why we can't coexist. It doesn't really matter any more. You know you are and always will be welcome in my world, and the tug of war is over'.

She leaned forward; her breath had an edge of gin.

'Find your own world, Lynda. Your own person. Your own love'.

Luigi had emerged from the car and was standing anxiously on the drive, as if expecting to be summoned and smacked at any moment. She pecked my cheek again and left without looking back or waving. She never waved.

It is full morning now, and a full Jurassic morning, breeze, big, big sky, the whole awesome miracle of light, shade and spectacle which absorbs me totally even after more than thirty years. It overwhelms me; unlike my father throwing himself into it and my mother manipulating it for her purposes, it reduces me to a scurrying creature like a little beach crab, rushing about its nondescript business as if the energy spent could somehow supply it with significance. Even as I choose the most comfortable seat on the balcony, where my father could spend hours in contemplation or in fervent discussion with his agent or various other hangers on and pseudo-lovers, and reflect again on the phenomenon of this all now being mine, I know much of me is still the pawn I became after my mother's departure. I divided my time between them, taking care of the routine of my father's life like a business manager and visiting my mother to wade my way through the Luigis, Toms, Leos and Jean-Claudes and be introduced to her arty restaurant critic and travel guide friends, feeding off her contacts as I equally shamelessly fed off my father's acolytes and admirers with their retrospectives, profiles and Sunday supplements. One night after a few drinks too many, the frequency of such nights increasing as her time away from my father lengthened, my mother saw a lavishly presented piece of mine featuring both his art and her food and leered at me, 'well, you may be a leech, darling, but you're a very versatile one'. She saw herself as living the life he had denied her, but the truth was that she never replaced him; the admiring men around her became older and more sophisticated, but she had little passion for any of them.

I go and dress myself fully; even in high summer, the beach can be raw at this time of day, indifferent as my father could be to it, and I have none of his bohemianism when it comes to clothing anyway. Like my mother, I do everything by a kind of invisible but defined handbook; like my father, I spend time drifting about waiting for things to occur to me.

But lately, when I walk from the house, I know with a kind of exhausted fatalism where I will finish up, however circuitous and inventive the route, and sure enough, within the hour I am at the spot where I found him, seven months ago, stretched along the sand like one of his more pessimistic works. His face was very uncharacteristically pale, his head stretched back as if making some last appeal to someone or something, and in a thin t-shirt and a rough pair of old khaki shorts, some kind of standing joke he had with Lewis, I noticed just how spare and worn his calves, arms and thighs had become. I had badgered him constantly about health checks, about the cigars and the half-tumblers of whisky or brandy, the lunch time benders with contemporaries as well as the still quite plentiful stream of hangers on and genuine admirers, both male and female, who apologetically asked to be admitted to his world for a while. It was early in the morning, similar to now. His guests had gone, or rather been chased out of the house by me; I had at least advanced to a rather more effective self-assertion. He was sixty two years old.

I did the necessary calls on my phone, but I knew the futility of it; he was already dead, the initial heart attack compounded by a following two, as if the Jurassic had finally decided to absorb him completely and dismiss the remaining competition. Not only had he destroyed his health, he'd exhausted both his body and his mind in the impossible effort to reproduce anything and everything conceived by his imagination.

He left me everything, absolutely everything. My mother did not contest the will; they had been divorced for over fifteen years by then. Neither did she come to the funeral; 'all those hangers on, pseudo-intellectuals and his various dreadful floosies; I just couldn't bear it, darling. I'd do or say something I probably wouldn't regret, but you might'.

I move away from that little patch of shingle where his life ended and wonder why I keep returning compulsively to it. I look from it to my distant house and back. Sudden decisions arrived in my life some time ago, as I handled his; who to trust, who not to trust, exhibitions probably worthwhile, exhibitions likely to be exploitative, even daily choices of how he could be made to eat something or take rest. Like a daily drum beat sometimes, bang, bang, bang; phone calls here, internet there, reading papers and magazines to check the coverage of him, keeping tabs of those who were taking cuts from his work, even including Lewis, who I neither liked nor trusted, with the disturbing contradiction between his ingratiating smile and wolf-like eyes. It did actually emerge in time that Lewis had sold some of his work at higher prices than he'd reported to my father and I, once I was able to get past the smokescreen my father's friendship for him put in front of me. However, the fact that he didn't figure in the will at all suggests my father wasn't as fooled as he'd seemed to be.

This particular sudden decision, standing on a beach familiar to me since childhood, is a momentous one in my life, and clicks away in my mind like so many dominoes falling. It's time for me to leave here, this, him totally and absolutely. Sell the place and all his work in it, apart from a private collection of my own favourites, and gather so much money and resources to myself that my constricted life, mesmerised and captured by the two of them, can start to gather some momentum of its own. Perhaps my own arts magazine; perhaps the editorship of someone else's; perhaps even my own publishing company. And who knows, perhaps wealth and prestige might finally produce a partner I can see seriously as an equal and who doesn't immediately pale into dwarfish insignificance in comparison with my redoubtable if incompatible parents.

Yes, there will be more hours of the wolf, I don't doubt, with bitter tastes of where I've been and insidious worries of where I might be going, brutally vivid memories of him and his more obliging admirers, around the house and along the shore, and the awesome spectacle of her Boudicca-light domination of her kitchens and her staff. I will wake to find my efforts paling into hamster on wheel insignificance beside theirs; I will wake yearning for the audible grumble of the Jurassic Coast; I will wake beside whoever and wonder how and why he has arrived in my life. But the story will finally be mine, not theirs.

By the time I am sitting down on my own personal balcony enjoying a pot of filtered coffee, I have already arranged for the house to be put on the market and his remaining work to go into secure storage. I am the soldier who saw out the war, and if I have emerged as a ruthlessly efficient creature, it's because that's how I've managed to survive. Perhaps, even perhaps, I am now the wolf whose hour it is.

THE LAMPEDUSA PASSAGE

It would be fair to say I was born with a silver spoon was in my mouth, even if the silver had an acidic edge. My father was already well on his way to his first billion, though I grew up distinctly hazy as to what actually made him his money; it seemed that he bought things and sold things, and each deal made him richer, year on year. As his oldest and, as it turned out, only son, he did try to explain the 'guts of the business' to me when he thought I was old enough, and because my schools reported to him that I was intelligent and could learn quickly, he decided this would be when I was eleven years old and starting secondary school. I tried to take an intelligent interest, but the whole business of business struck me as both morbidly self-interested and impenetrably boring. I was my mother's son, and had no shame about it. My French mother, whose grace and beauty had so entranced my father, took her greatest pleasures from the study of languages; she was a professional linguist and an inveterate traveller, and I followed her in both ways from childhood. By my mid-teens, my father was behaving as if my mother had stolen me away from him, his golden heir, the Prince of the Sanderson empire. Why I had no brothers and sisters, I don't know; they didn't tell me and I didn't dare ask, as even tentative enquiries met with evasion or even hostility.

My father insisted that, as he was the providing source of my comfort and expensive education, my duty was to prepare myself in every possible way for my inheritance, his business empire. It wasn't actually true that he was the sole provider for me; my mother was comfortably off in her own right, and she did contribute – I knew that, and I knew my father knew that, but playing them off against each other was a route which I had decided fairly early on in life not to follow. The tensions between them grew through my late childhood and teens, but I was self-contained enough not to allow myself to become their matrimonial football. And I admired and esteemed both of them, if in different ways. It isn't just parents whose knowledge of their offspring accumulates over the years; it works the other way too.

The first intimations of crisis came when I was sixteen and choosing my A level subjects. I chose French, Spanish and Italian; French was a giveaway; I'd grown up bilingual, thanks to my mother, and my extensive travels around Europe had made the other languages equally accessible. My father, of course, wanted me to do Economics, Business Studies and Law, all 'things which are actually of some use'. We were sitting in his great spaceship of an office at the time, overlooking the City of London. I always tried very hard to treat him with respect; he had never been cruel to me, mentally or physically, and I had been given a wonderful education with every possible facility, but now and then, he stung me out of my general passivity towards him.

'So speaking the languages which, including my native English, are spoken by almost the entire world is not of any practical use, Dad?'

He did the stare he uses on his underlings, but that had long since failed to intimidate me and he knew it. He was my dad, not my boss. I grinned, and he found my grin infectious. He smiled in spite of himself.

'Yes, it has its uses, of course, but for running a large and complex business empire?'

'Well, if I was doing that, I would need to travel the world, wouldn't I, and I might just be able to understand what they're talking about, eh Dad?'

I grinned again, and he sat shaking his head.

'Always have to have the last word. Just like your mother'.

We'd negotiated that one as we had others, but my growing feeling was yes, I had obligations to do the right thing by my parents, but that meant both of them, and it wasn't just about obligations, it was about rights, including my right to become the person I chose to be and needed to be.

The crunch came in 2011, in the late summer after I'd received my A level results. It was three months after my eighteenth birthday, the onset of adulthood, and, as I saw it, freedom. My father was cruising the Mediterranean in his big yacht Adventurer, for business purposes, of course, every bit as much as leisure. I had secured a good university place for my linguistic studies and already had formidable reading lists to deal with before my first term. However, my hard work and success, I thought, deserved a holiday and my father did his guests, and his family, very well.

The Adventurer made its stately way into the harbour of the Sardinian capital Cagliari with the usual groups of tourists and locals staring at it drifting by with varying degrees of amazement and envy. I was entranced; Cagliari, with a settlement history dating back to Neolithic times and with Carthaginian, Roman and Byzantine dwellings layered below it, struck me as lovely in a magnificently disorganised way, its orange and brown rectangular buildings climbing the hill behind the harbour.

Dinner in the evening was on the big sundeck as usual. The stewards had stocked up with

Cagliari's finest, and everyone felt so good by the time my father was swishing his brandy around his glass that I was as intoxicated by the atmosphere as the wine.

'Next stop will be Malta', my father, Richard Sanderson the tycoon, said, his handsome if now liberally grey-flecked head rising to face his guests, and the hypnotic light blue eyes which I had inherited alive with good living. 'In case you were wondering. I have a few business pals in Valetta, who let's say rather enjoy the relaxed tax regime on offer'.

There were a few of Dad's business associates on this part of the cruise, and everyone sniggered dutifully, including me, even though I wasn't sure what I was sniggering at.

'You'll need to watch out for these damn migrant boats, with this war in Libya', said a hefty, ponderous man on my father's right, whose name was Lloyd, as far as I could remember. The cruises always included these 'business associates', and I didn't pay much attention to them, to my father's irritation; his son and heir should be taking an interest in everyone associated with his father's business. I did at least try to converse with them occasionally.

'Clandestini', I said.

'What?' Lloyd's eyes shot round at me, then he remembered I was the boss's son. 'Paul?'

'Clandestini. That's what the Italians call them. Illegals. Though refugees might be better'.

Lloyd gazed at me blankly.

'Really. Right, Paul. Well, whatever they're called, they're a bloody nuisance, especially in the night, when the chances are they're not carrying any lights'.

My father took a swig of brandy and grinned.

'Well, if we do clout into one, we'd be doing the Italians a favour!'

Dutiful sniggering again, though this time, I didn't join in. The remark was of the kind which Dad would not make when

Mum was on the boat, as she wouldn't be on this cruise until the last two weeks, because of her own business interests. Facing him across the table, she would say 'that's uncalled for, Richard', while around the boat, the company would marvel at someone daring to talk to the one and only Sir Richard Sanderson in such a way.

When Mum was not with them, Dad would usually invite me and some favoured business associates to his own luxuriously appointed cabin. I sometimes went, out of a sense of duty, but I didn't much care for it, as I would be pressurised to drink too much or listen to subjects which made me uneasy. I was often out of my depth and sometimes downright bored with many of the subjects the company tended to talk about. My approaching degree gave me the study option, and I used it as often as I thought I could get away with.

'Sorry, Dad. University reading lists and all that. They don't give you degrees, do they?'

My father gave me the surly nod typical of his response to such requests. But it was a kind of acquiescence.

Not for the first time, I returned to my cabin a little ashamed of myself, because I'd already decided on the late night 'skinny dip' which gave me the freedom and relaxation not always easy during the day. I felt old enough to indulge in such activities without asking permission, but my instinct that Dad would object led me to a certain amount of subterfuge.

I stripped in my cabin. I'd discovered the joy of swimming naked at school, with a small lake in the grounds regarded as the senior boys' territory. It was simple enough to open the cabin door and look either way, like crossing the road, before running across the deck and launching myself from the railings on the starboard side of the boat. Returning was usually just as easy, with steps up the side of the boat and anyone passing easily heard. I was luxuriating in the water in seconds, and the frustrations of the day fell rapidly away.

The Adventurer had moored with nothing on the starboard side between it and the open sea. I swam steadily seawards, on my usual basis of twenty minutes out, a pause to enjoy the view, and twenty minutes back. My pause showed me an intensely beautiful pattern of Cagliari lights against the translucent blue of the sky. I languished about and relished the beautiful night. By the time I climbed back up the boat's side, the dip has done its job; I felt relaxed and unwound.

In the morning, Adventurer made her graceful way out of Cagliari heading east, and I had an easy day of it, with costumed swimming and some language work. After dinner, I excused myself again from my father's late night business booze; this time his nod was more disgruntled and doubting. The boat had anchored for the night in mid-sea, as it did sometimes to get away from the noise, fuss and inquisitive media on shore, and swimming with no company but sea, sky and moonlight was again too good an idea to resist.

Stepping tentatively out of my cabin, I heard my father and the boat's captain talking, but I couldn't hear what they were saying. I hovered uncertainly. Footsteps started heading in my direction. The threat of losing my swim panicked me. I scampered across to dive from the rail into the sea.

As ever, the easy caress of the water settled me down, and I struck out strongly and pushed on for longer than usual. When I turned to enjoy the view, a ghastly fact became apparent, much as I tried to dismiss it as optical illusion. The Adventurer seemed to be moving away. I shut my eyes in concentration, and when I looked again, the boat's lights were quite clearly further away.

For a long, uncomfortable moment, I couldn't accept that such a thing could happen. Then, realising that my chances of reaching the boat were disappearing, I struck out at high speed towards it. But after a pause for breath, I looked again, and it was gone.

My desire to scream and cry seized and left me in almost the same moment. For the time being, I had to believe the situation was retrievable. But there were no visible shore lights, and I couldn't remember where the boat had been in relation to the shore. I struck out towards where I thought land was. Time passed, and my limbs began to resist, slightly at first, and then more heavily. I am a good swimmer, but not in the Channel swimmer league, and I got to the point where even pausing and treading water was sapping my energy.

I breathed deeply. O.K., it was odds against, but I was the son of a tycoon father and a formidable mother, and I would give it a go, even if I died in the attempt.

Half an hour later, there were still no lights visible and I knew I couldn't go on much longer. The night was colder than the previous one and the water was chilling me to the bone. I was not far from despair when creaking noises and disjointed shouts suddenly sounded to my right, and a boat appeared no more than a hundred yards away. No lights were visible except one weak lamp, and although it was not much bigger than a barge, it seemed to be carrying at least fifty or sixty people.

The boat drifted towards me. Voices came at me in strangely disjointed bursts. I could detect snatches of French, Italian and what sounded like Arabic, and some of their talk suggested that they were arguing about whether to rescue me at all. I decided on Italian.

'Per favore. Aiutami. Sto annegando. Per favore', I shouted into the night, wondering at the cracked, desperate sound of my voice.

'Zitto, accidenti a te. Lui è solo un ragazzo'.

Damn you, he's only a boy, and I had no argument, if such reasoning meant rescue.

A large, aggressive middle-aged woman had elbowed herself to the side of the boat, with two other women beside her. Two younger men nearby shook their heads doubtfully, but made to help. Being hauled naked out of the water by a predominantly female group was not an experience which had any precedent in my life, but I didn't care. I heard a few distinctly coarse remarks in Italian as well, but I didn't care about them either. I sat with my back against the side of the boat, my arms clutched round me for warmth. The people started to look pityingly at what must have been my deathly paleness and seemed to appreciate how serious the situation was; one woman handed me a rough, thick blanket, hairy on my bare skin and smelling powerfully of animals, and I wrapped it around me gratefully. When a young man also handed me a long blue anorak, their kindness and my exhaustion overwhelmed me and I wept quietly into my smelly blanket.

As warmth and strength returned slowly, my curiosity began to overcome my tiredness. The woman who had been my main rescuer spoke for them; most of the people nearby seemed to be related to her.

'We are Libyans, my family', she said, in her precise but accented Italian. 'My mother was brought up in the days of Italian Libya, and taught us the language. She always said my grandmother was Italian, but we couldn't prove it. Now we flee the chaos and death in our Libya. My son Halim was shot down in the street and his wife fled to her own family. His son Dhaamin, my grandson, is on the boat with us'.

She pointed to the young man who had handed me the coat; he looked about the same age as me. I held out my hand to him, and after a moment's bewilderment, he shook it.

'My name is Parveen', the woman continued. 'What's left of my family gathered what money we had and fled Libya; after much trial and suffering, we reached Mahdia in Tunisia, where we met men who said they could arrange a boat for us to go to Lampedusa, an Italian island, away from death and persecution. We gave them everything we had; we got this wreck, whose ancient engine has now broken down and whose timbers are so old that she is sinking beneath us'.

I looked down at my feet; sure enough, the water had visibly risen.

'These men are crooks, bastards and…' Parveen used a word outside my vocabulary, but I understood the extremity of it.

A shout from someone at the front of the ship made everyone turn. Boat lights were approaching. They stopped briefly, and then came on. For a moment, I was unsure, but as it came closer, I recognised the unmistakable shape of the Adventurer. Keeping only the coat around me, I stepped up to the prow of the ship and stood on the edge of the wooden rail. The people around me seemed to back away, gazing at the hulking shape of the yacht, now only a few hundred metres away.

'Dad!' I screamed. 'Get a line on to us! This boat is sinking! These people saved my life!'

My father's voice boomed across the gap.

'Paul! Swim to us, son! It's no distance! Swim over!'

'These people? Dad?'

'Yes, yes. We will attend to it, boy. Come back over'.

Giving the coat back to Dhaamin, whose eyes wouldn't meet mine, I plunged off the rail and swam across to the boat. As soon as I was on the deck, someone gave me a huge towel and directed me towards my cabin. I could already sense the boat starting to move.

'Dad? What's happening? Dad, I told you – those people saved my life –'

'Below, Paul, please. We will talk in your cabin, not shout at each other on deck'.

In my cabin, as I dressed, I felt the boat accelerating quickly away. Sitting on the bed, almost in tears, I looked up at my father in anger and bewilderment.

'Dad, really, seriously, are you going to go off and leave those people to drown?'

'No, of course not. The captain has informed the Italian coastguard; he did so before you came over. They were only thirty minutes out of Lampedusa. They will be intercepted well in time. And you, Paul, are in no position to take the moral high ground with me.'

'What do you mean?'

He leant towards me, the blue eyes flashing with anger.

'You lied to me. Consistently. Supposedly studying, then swimming off into the night. Night swimming isn't advisable in these waters. If it wasn't for an alert crew member having seen you jump off the rail, we might never have known. As it is, we have had to explore a lot of sea to find you'.

'My fault, is it? And why exactly did you suddenly shoot off in the middle of the night?'

'One of the men I needed to see in Malta was leaving earlier'.

'You left me because you had a business proposition?'

Dad's temper finally snapped. He turned away and marched towards the cabin window.

'I didn't know you had been fool enough to go off into the bloody water, did I?'

I felt myself rocking backwards and forwards, half crying. His more tender side yes, he had one – came to the fore; he placed a hand gently on my shoulder.

'I'll send you a hot drink, son. I think you're still in shock. Try to get some sleep. We'll talk everything over tomorrow'.

I never knew what happened to the hot drink; perhaps he looked in and decided not to bother. Waking hours later, after dreams of eternal water and hands holding my naked body up for general inspection, the need for rest overcame everything else. But as soon as the morning came, I knew a confrontation was now inevitable. For Dad and I, kicking the can down the road once again was not, as he would call it, an option.

And he obviously felt the same. He saw his businessman in the morning, and after lunch, he took me to the docks. I saw the refugees' boat, with several others, half sunk in the bay. In and around a large wooden boathouse nearby sat or lay several hundred people. Dad's car drove to within a few hundred yards and I emerged as he sat watching. I tried to see Parveen and Dhaamin, and waved furiously. A few policemen looked across at me as if at a madman, and none of the people dotted around the boathouse responded. A large military-looking boat was approaching the boathouse, and a coldness descended on me as my suspicions rose that those people were about to be taken straight back. I stood next to my father's big Mercedes gazing at the old boathouse; physically close, those people and I might as well have been on two different planets. And the policemen's hands unsubtly placed on their gun holsters made clear the probable result of me trying to get any closer.

Leaving the Adventurer for cleaning and maintenance, Dad and I spent the night in a five star hotel in Valetta, with splendid views of Marsamxett Harbour and Manoel Island, and now in the far distance, an old boathouse.

After dinner, we looked out over the Mediterranean, and I wondered how many more boats were out there trying to struggle out of their hellish world to our becalmed one. The whole experience had given me a determination and certainty that I had never felt before.

'You're in the business of making money, Dad', I said. He was on his second large brandy, and a little misty-eyed; he knew what this was leading to. 'I'm not getting hypocritical about that; I've benefited from it well enough, as have quite a few other people, I don't doubt. But I have the means to communicate with people, and while I'm young enough to still have ideals about reducing the great gaping inequality of people and wealth which this whole thing has demonstrated to me all too clearly, my course when I've graduated will be to work for the U.N. or another international organisation. I can't be what you want me to be, Dad, even if I was capable of it, which I'm not'.

He turned from profile to full on, and I saw, to my grief, tears glistening in his eyes.

'You might find it difficult to believe, Paul, but I once felt much as you do. I was travelling the world, making contacts, and it became all too clear that everywhere was much the same. Come to terms with the powerful, tread carefully, and you can make life comfortable and protected for your wife and family. But only if you arrive at a position of power yourself. Do what you will, son, and I will back you in every way I can. But don't be surprised if you feel differently when you have a family of your own'.

So my right to choose my own way without being steamrollered into my father's was granted to me. I graduated well in 2014, and starting working for the U.N. as a translator. In late 2015, I met a doctor called Jeannette working for Medecins Sans Frontieres in one of the French-speaking African countries. We had a child in September 2016 and called him Richard, after my father and one of Jeannette's uncles, pronounced the English or French ways depending on where we are. Both grandmothers expressed delight as well as a preference for Richard growing up with married parents, and for that and a few other reasons, Jeannette and I married in 2018.

My father has offered me a post as Sanderson's 'Head of Ethics', with considerable power to control investments and activities according to ethical principles. It is effective power, with a very good wage and opportunities to travel the world. Jeannette is happy for me to take it, but she does not feel able to leave M.S.F. for at least another three years, meaning she will continue to work in dangerous areas and my son will be brought up mostly by trained nannies. Because I am multi-lingual, the U.N. doesn't want me to leave either.

In many ways, I feel once again as adrift and naked as that night in the Mediterranean. My father has now given me two weeks, or he will need to appoint someone else.

So what do I do? What would you do?

FIRST NIGHT

Teachers' claims to fame tend to be few and far between; it isn't a job anyone does for the glory and kudos of it. But there are moments, usually associated with particular pupils, which can become treasures, invisible but very real memories of stand out moments.

A certain gentleman now in his mid-forties used to attend the school where I worked at the time. His name is well-known and he has told me himself that he wouldn't strenuously object to my naming him in my story, but I took a clue from the 'strenuously' qualification, and in any case, his name and fame are only relevant in so far as they show how most acting careers get started and the price usually very young people pay for their success.

I'll call him Tom Martin and I'll call me John Hepworth. I had been teaching English and Drama for ten years at the time and at last beginning to believe I was actually passably good at it. Teaching does take time and persistence.

It was pantomime night, hopefully a good night out for all involved, but a lot of work for the producer and director, i.e. me. I'd taken it over four years before from a much-loved local legend, Margaret Field, on her retirement, and I could only wonder at how she had managed to keep on with such a project into her sixties.

Twenty minutes before curtain up, I went to notify the Head, Ralph Hayman, as requested, that we would only be about ten minutes late with curtain up. He had a local politico in tow,

Councillor Ron Mitchell, full time head gardener somewhere, part-time councillor and pain in the neck. With the festive season very close, Ralph was trying to look benevolent and avuncular, but his spectacles and thin frame kept the detached academic look on him however hard he tried. I smiled at Ralph and nodded civilly at Councillor Mitchell.

'About twenty minutes, Mr. Hayman, to the festive fun and frolics'.

'Yes. Smashing. Everything running smoothly in your capable hands, no doubt, Mr. Hepworth. You know the Councillor, I take it?'

'Oh, yes, old friends', I say, shaking hands and praying to be forgiven.

I felt their eyes on my retreating back and heard Ralph saying something else about how well everything would go. I wondered, a little irritably, why he needed to work so hard to convince himself and the councillor. I'd been doing it for four years, for heaven's sake.

I sneaked a peak into the hall and saw my noble spouse Susan as in Sue, the sexiest Maths teacher in the world, in unflustered charge of making sure children and some pensioners from a local home were not coming together in any peace-threatening situations.

Back stage, the spectacle was familiar enough to me but would probably be seen as pretty bizarre to most people; teenagers of both sexes costumed and made up in various spectacular outfits without – and this is the real miracle – apparent embarrassment. The silver-glittering creature in the blonde wig next to me was just about recognisable as Alan Dodds. I realised that we had an important absentee, in Tom Martin, Buttons himself.

'Where's Tom?'

'In the changing room, sir. Chunder – I mean, being sick, I think'.

My inner panic button sounded immediately. Tom had told me confidentially, when I first picked him for the part, of his sometimes turbulent internal arrangements, his 'unpredictable' stomach. He wasn't stupid enough to drink, but a certain amount of comfort eating could well have been going on. Sirens sounding. The idea wasn't to send kids out to die on stage, and certainly not at the age of fourteen.

'O.K., Alan. Have you spoken to him?'

Alan was a good kid in almost every respect, but not necessarily greatly gifted in coping with the unexpected. After about thirty seconds of his mouth opening and closing silently like a meditative carp, I decided immediate action was our only chance.

'Follow me'.

We arrived at the changing room door and I asked Alan to stay just outside; this conversation with Tom needed to be just me and him. Alan stood there resolutely, Prince Charming on sentry duty like a fallen aristo.

I reflected ruefully for about the thousandth time on the unpredictability of kids. Tom Martin was a gifted boy, and generally rock solid reliable, in spite of his dodgy stomach; he always made rehearsals on time, he always knew his stuff on time. He'd come to us with a glowing primary school record and been in productions since the age of eleven. I'd been very careful with him, but after a long debate with Jen and others, I'd decided to give him a major leading role at the age of fourteen, partly because it was a 'only' a pantomime and simple compared to some of the other stuff he'd done, though not as the lead, and partly because he seemed increasingly like one of the very few who might actually make it professionally without being condemned to endless days waiting for the phone to ring or washing dishes in Burger King.

As Buttons, in rehearsals, he'd carried the show, being as much a natural for comedy as for the rest of it.

I banged open the changing room door —you had to give it a hefty bang it to open it properly, such intelligent design in a school — and a half-gurgled response sounded from the shower area away to the right, followed by words to the effect that if I was 'Doddo again', I could go away and do something unmentionable to myself.

Loud cough. 'It's Mr. Hepworth, Tom'.

A clump, a gulp and a shuffle. His face and half-jacketed torso appeared slowly around the side of the shower wall, and I fought to avoid a highly undiplomatic grin. His Buttons costume was curious to begin with, Helen Pearson's page boyish interpretation of what Buttons, who's supposed to be a scullery lad, would wear. The red and blue jacket with odd silver buttons — hence the name, thinks Helen — was now open to the waist, and some of the chest besmirched with something dubious. His scarlet cap was in a corner where, I suspected, he had thrown it.

I had reassured myself about having been too tolerant of Helen Pearson's costumes with the thought that youth can get away with just about anything and, in Tom's case, he had the talent to turn even apparent disadvantage around. In the dress rehearsal, he'd got an unscripted laugh out of just gazing doubtfully at a button and trying to remove it.

'I can't do it, sir. I just can't do it'.

I sat down on a bench and motioned him over.

'Well, before the pantomime goes completely down the pan, Tom, you can at least tell me what we've done to deserve it. Prince Charming's on guard'.

He reverted to child mode, like teens do, and sat looking sullenly at his feet, ditto. He retched briefly but controlled himself.

'I'm scared. I'm bricking it, pardon me, sir. Matthews and his gang are out there. You know well enough what they're like, sir. And I look a right pillock, let's face it.'

I was, and I suppose I sounded it, genuinely mystified.

'Tom, you've been on stage countless times, in all sorts of outfits. What's the problem with this one?'

'This one, sir, carries the whole show; if I die, it dies. I feel – what should I call it – in over my head, you know?'

I sighed heavily. A little stagey, but we have our tricks too.

'Well, no-one's going to **make** you do it, Tom'.

He did a shape change, sitting up and backing his shoulders; the child disappearing again.

'No, I know, sir. You're always fair, I know'.

One of those moments, I suppose, when they notice you're there; the dummy in the distance, waving and smiling, is taking shape as another adult. Opportunity knocked.

'We've all been there, Tom, teachers as well, especially starting out. Young teachers waking up sweating, thinking about the homicidal bunch of teenage thugs who are going to have them for breakfast tomorrow.'

I found myself remembering my earlier teaching days very vividly. He heard the catch in my voice and his eyes joined me properly at last.

'Deep breaths in the staff loo, then get out there before you stop to think about it again. And that's just classes of kids, not whole audiences'.

'That's not a line that's making things any better here, sir'. Another little retch.

'Tom'. The eyes turned and he was, he really was, listening.

'I think you just might be a real actor. Nothing is guaranteed, and you must know it won't be easy, but I feel much more positive about your chances than most. You have natural ability, fact not flattery, and it would be a crying shame for you not to do something with it. But if you're sensitive enough to do it, you're sensitive enough to feel it. It's a two-sided coin. Cheers in your ears; throwing up in the showers. Enjoy the one, pay the other.

Or what – hide and watch the world go by, life without risk or challenge? A swimmer afraid of the water? A sportsman afraid of losing? Not much of an existence. I don't think, anyway'.

So it came, Tom Martin's crossroads. Precisely identified growing up moments are a bit of myth with kids; it's a gradual process, as it's bound to be. But now and then, there can be an event, a turning point, which can be pointed at as a real change happening. His head stayed down; for a moment, I thought he was going to cry at the prospect of a lifetime of trying to hold his stomach down and his confidence up, and I suspected he was doing that thing I did as a boy, sort of crying inside.

He sat there, occasionally making odd shuffling sounds, as if he could cry if he tried, and sometimes nodding his head up and down to himself. Somehow, we were not embarrassed; a temporary truce had been declared in awkward teacher-pupil land. Perhaps a next step which might work could be bantering humour; it could be infectious with them, optimistic gestures against all challenges.

'Then there's the question of what Belinda will do to you'.

Belinda Crowthorne, alias Cinderella, was the sweetest of sweet kids off stage, but a veritable Gorgon in greasepaint with anyone who mucked her about on it.

The point registered; to my intense if hidden amusement, his knees moved together.

'Oh, God, yes. Wouldn't she just'.

He smiled to himself, and a button had been pressed somehow, because he got up, took the jacket off, went to a sink and rinsed and dried himself down. Then he put the shirt back on, fastened it, silver buttons and all, and replaced the hat with a grimace into the mirror.

The merciless door banged again and Prince Charming appeared, now looking a great deal more like a puzzled kid with a wig on.

'Tom, squeaky bum time, pal. Are we doing this, or what?'

He just nodded, to my amazement, and they headed off. Yet another door bang sounded.

I went into the shower, and managed to get rid of the remaining incrimination without soaking myself. He didn't need that facing him when he came back.

When Buttons first emerged, Matthews and sidekicks contorted themselves in very unfestive laughter. Buttons narrowed his eyes, pursed his lips and flicked a camp finger off his silver button at them, adding yet another unscripted laugh and allowing the enemies of the Matthews' gang to loudly relish the moment. And so the show continued; Buttons word-perfect throughout, and with a few added bits all of his own.

A star, I thought, is born. Quieter they may be, but teachers have their moments too.

MILLIE ELLIOT – LEARNING THE DRILL

Millie banged open the front door and announced 'Mum, I'm home' at the top of her voice, immediately following it with 'at long last' under her breath.

'Just going to get changed', she said, shouting towards wherever Mum was.

Reaching the sanctuary of her bedroom, Millie reflected that even here, her own most personal space, the world was the way it was rather than the way she wanted it to be. She flung the ballet bag – leotard, towel, shoes, the whole paraphernalia – into the back of her wardrobe. Millie was now fifteen and had been going to ballet classes since she was six. Physically, it showed; she was lean and athletic, with jet black hair cut short for the practicalities of movement. But she did not feel as keen on ballet as she used to be.

It still surrounded her on all sides. Millie thought of her bedroom as having official and unofficial bits; the pictures and posters were all official, meaning they were about ballet. There was a two foot high picture of Viviana Durante dancing in Romeo and Juliet, a Principal Dancer good enough to become the Royal Ballet's Principal at the age of 21; Millie's admiration and respect was boundless.

Further along the wall were a few stills from 'Black Swan', starring Natalie Portman, which had produced Mother's uncertain smile once again. Mum knew the story line of Black Swan, where the dancer is so pushed by her mother and her director that she unleashes dark forces within herself. Millie just said that the dance poses were sensational, reflecting grumpily to herself that even when she tried to be good, fault was found.

The biggest picture was of Melissa Hamilton and Carlos Acosta in Agon, Melissa who had worked her way up after early rejection – 'she really is a model for you, Millie', Dad had said – next to Acosta, 'undoubtedly now the best male dancer in the world', according to Miss Cooper, as she was when her dancers weren't doing what she described as 'the business', Roz when they were.

Acosta wasn't the only semi-naked man on the wall – ballet dancers were allowed – with large stills from Ivan Putrov's 'Men in Motion', which also had Daniel Proietto and the 21-year-old Sergei Polunin from the Royal Ballet. And, of course, there were stills dotted here and there from the productions Millie and her friends had been in, with the school and the dance group, and a few cups and medals. Millie knew her 'official' bedroom was full of achievement, culture and artistic excellence, which was fine, except that she felt increasingly detached from it all, as an alien world she no longer inhabited.

Sure enough, she was soon reaching into the divan drawer of her bed and bringing two enlarged and detailed pictures, the first of a heavy duty stoper, a piece of machinery which could shear its way through just about every substance known to man, and the second of a fully illustrated blasthole drill, its size doing full justice to the power of it.

The crucial word, Millie thought to herself as she contemplated these awesome engineering achievements, is power. Sheer power, not vaguely held by some performance in front of people, but power held in your hand, to do anything, anywhere, whatever the substance or the obstacle. This was the kind of power which made a difference when people got trapped, when accidents happened, when obstacles were in the way of whatever was needed to keep the world going or keep people alive. Real living power, for whoever controlled it. 'Most of the effective power is still in the hands of men', she had heard Roz and some of her friends say more than once. She sometimes wondered whether they meant it literally.

But Dad, who lectured in Dance and Drama at a famous college, would never be convinced that drilling and tunnelling were legitimate occupations for girls, even those who admired so much the Channel Tunnel and Cross Rail projects, amongst others, which did so much to aid people's transport and communication needs. She could remember in detail their first argument on the subject. He'd seen her looking at this very same stoper picture; she was less careful in those days. He seemed puzzled and even a little amused.

'A strange recreation for a ballerina', he said. She was thirteen then; the school had visited an exhibition of tunnelling and drilling equipment, where she'd started picking up brochures and pictures. Naively, she thought, looking back, she mentioned her thinking about power. Power in the hands.

'Oh, dear'. Long, paternal sigh. 'I think the main reason why men are the ones who handle those machines is physical strength; I can't see any great skill would be involved. Any competent engineer or driller could use them'.

She looked at him with her mouth open for so long that his face was silently shaped into the word 'what?' by the time she found her speech.

'First, Dad,' she said, 'these machines don't need enormous physical strength to handle them; they're too sensitive for that. You can release enormous power with them; you don't need enormous power to use them. Second, that's why they do need skill, and a lot of it, if you're not going to hack bits off yourself and everyone else. It's like shooting an arrow, except much more complicated; you don't just do it with your eyes or your hands, you do it with your brain and your skills. And third, no, anyone certainly can't do it, strength or not; you have to have been trained to use these things and have the certificates to prove it'.

'Well, there you are, then'.

'Where am I then?'

Another long sigh emerged from her father.

'You could only be trained by working with men, in tunnels and other dirty, dangerous places, sweaty and half naked men; most distasteful'.

'Dad, by the end of a dance practice session, all of us, boys and girls, are sweaty and half naked, especially on a warm day. What's the difference?'

Backed into a corner, Mr. Elliott instantly turned to a different tack.

'Mining, drilling, those activities are too dangerous, Millie. You must see that'.

Millie sat right up in her armchair.

'An entrechat, Dad, you know what it is, well enough. You have to skip your legs across in front of your calves rapidly, and then go into an ascent. If you mis-time it when both your legs are off the ground, you could easily fall and break your leg. People have. You know *grande battement* as well; flinging one leg way out in front of you, also **after** you've achieved the movement of getting both feet off the ground. For both girls and boys, the groin consequences can be potentially disastrous – '

'Millie, please'.

'Oh, right, yes. Distasteful, is it? No need to worry about dancers are doing to themselves when you're sat watching them, is there? Just don't tell me it's not dangerous. It is'.

'Well, almost anything physical is dangerous when you don't know what you're doing'.

'Exactly!' Millie said triumphantly. Her father looked at her blankly.

'When I was six and you started taking me to dance classes, Dad –'

'Now don't make me the big bad wolf, Millie. You were clamouring to go at the time'.

'Yes, sure. But what you like at the age of six and what you like at the age of fifteen aren't the same thing, are they? Were they with you?'

This was a question to be carefully ducked.

'Millie, you are very good at it! Everyone says so, including Roz Cooper, and she's not one for false praise, by any means. You could do well'.

'I could be a member of a dance company; I might even make a living out of it. But it won't be the Royal Ballet, and I won't be a principal'.

'Well, no you won't, if you're defeated before you start. Look at Melissa Hamilton'.

'It's given me a lot of skills, Dad, and I'm grateful for that. It's taught me how to handle movement, how to understand my body, control it, get the most out of it. But highly refined physical skills can be used in a lot of jobs, without struggling on with impossible aims and turning yourself into a permanent cripple along the way'.

She'd had the last word then, and she'd usually had it in the two years since, the argumentsnrepeating themselves again and again until poor Mum had piggied in the middle to exhaustion. All the same, he was determined and he was still holding the purse strings. And yes, at fifteen and a dancer for nearly ten years, walking away was not going to be easy. She could imagine the guffawing voices and mocking faces of the male workforce standing between her and the beautiful machinery she longed to use and control, and compared to the enthusiastic applause of the audiences after performances, amateur as they may be, the prospect was undoubtedly a bit daunting.

A reckoning day inevitably had to come and it did. For once, all three of the family were in the living room watching the news, and an item came on about an ambitious tunnel scheme to drive the main road under an obstructive hill no more than three miles out of the city. Rock had fallen in a newly opened tunnel and eight drillers were trapped in an almost airless cave inside it. A disconsolate drilling crew were trying to look as if they knew what they were doing and keep the media people at bay.

'Our understanding is', said the reporter, 'that the rescue crews are having trouble with their drilling equipment; cutting through the now considerable piles of rubble separating them from the men. The trapped men have no light and very little air, and it is looking at the moment as if it might take more time than they have, though no-one is publicly saying so'.

'My God'. Mum had gone white; she was a sensitive soul.

'Those poor men will suffocate'.

Millie was later to regret her outburst, but her pent up frustrations seemed to burst in her like a broken dam.

'Shall I put on a tutu, then, Dad, and *demi-detourne* on over there? Don't worry, guys, your mates in there may be about to die, but you can watch me doing a special *ronde de jambe* for free, you lucky people'.

Her father got to his feet, and for a moment Millie thought that an embittered, rejoinder was about to come her way. Mum looked up at her husband with her usual apprehension.

'Now, Martin – ' she started to say, but he seemed to have decided on a question for Millie.

'I suppose you think you know, do you, what machine they're using?'

'In that place, with that narrowness of space and intensity of rock, almost certainly a Boomer T1 D, at the moment – nothing else would have the power'.

'And I suppose you have a diagram of it?'

'Yes, diagram and specifications'.

Millie was beginning to feel a little nervous herself.

'Well, get it, because we're going there. I know where that place is; I pass it regularly on one of my university visits. No more than twenty miles, I would say. I don't know whether either of us will be able to make any meaningful contribution – well, I certainly won't – but if nothing else, we might get the chance to see one of these mechanical contrivances you like so much in the flesh, as it were. I'm not stubborn-headed or narrow minded, Millie; I want you to understand that'.

She looked from one parent to the other, and noticed her mother's eyes had relaxed at last.

They were mostly silent in the car, though it was a more companionable silence than they'd had between them for some time. Martin Elliott was thinking about his school teaching experience, before higher education, and all those children, mostly girls, who wanted desperately to have the ability to dance to a professional standard, especially since the 'Strictly' series had started, and who never would have. Millie did, even if she wasn't going to be greatest diva of all time, and it had always seemed to him little short of criminal for her to waste it; her timing, her movement, her muscle and breathing control, were all excellent and seemingly natural gifts.

But what had suddenly occurred to Martin, surprising him as something which he perhaps should have thought of before, was the career of his brother Peter. From being a toddler onwards, Peter had been intrigued, even obsessed, with machinery, and his eventual qualification as an engineer was perhaps the most predictable career course in a family of one girl and three boys with next to nothing in common except some physical resemblances. He liked to think that Millie's dancing ability had been largely inherited from his own school athletics and gymnastics successes and her mother's gymnastics as well – they had actually met in a gymnastics hall. But genetic allocations weren't necessarily just from parents. If she had also acquired a talent from her uncle, why should she not also make use of that, and if a girl Hdid inherit engineering abilities, why should they be intimidated into not exploiting them in the way that boys did, in the way that Peter had, as a matter of course?

They arrived at the site; the shaft which went down into the tunnel had been cordoned off, so that no-one could get within a hundred yards. Clusters of very anxious people could do nothing but stand and wait, sometimes holding hands and giving each other consoling hugs. The policemen who were manning the cordon took time off occasionally to talk to people and keep them updated with progress in the mine. As a pall of silence was hanging over the site, the fact that the machinery was not working was all too abundantly obvious.

Martin and Millie were wondering how it might be possible for her to at least look at the huge Boomer drill when a helmeted man wondered towards the cordon. He walked slowly and a little painfully. Not more than fifty yards away from the cordon, the reason for his 'time out' became clear enough; even under the helmet, he looked exhausted. When he took the helmet off, his sweating brow and fatigue showed clearly.

Spasmodic enquiries started being fired at him from the cordon. For a moment, he turned his face away as if this was more than he could live with, then he seemed to make a particular effort and started to make such reassuring noises as he could. Having drifted to only about twenty yards away from the rope, he saw

Millie looking intently at her big picture of the Boomer, which identified its constituent parts very carefully. Millie looked up to see him watching her.

'It is one of these, isn't it?' she said.

'Yes, it is'. He came over to them, too curious to resist further investigation.

The ensuing ten minutes of conversation between Millie and the engineer might just as well have been in Chinese as far as Martin and the rest of the people gathered round were concerned, but the sense of what they were saying seemed to be that the man was ruefully acknowledging, being too weary and irritated for further pretences, that the drill was idle and they could not at this stage work out why; Millie, incredibly, seemed to be advancing possible theories. Eventually, the man looked at Millie directly and wonderingly.

'You have given me a few ideas. One or two of them I would and should have thought of myself if I hadn't been here for nearly thirty hours without sleep, but one in particular I would never have thought of, the one about the fuel flow malfunctioning in that tiny pipe or that reaction which neutralises a power source. I can't take you right to the accident site, you're too young, but we will now try a few things, and I'm going to arrange access for you to the office. We'll talk later'.

Two tense hours went by as Millie and Martin paced up and down, watching helmeted and very dirty men going up and down the lifts. Then there was suddenly a fuller, gutsier noise below and an unmistakable thin and scattered cheer emerged from the tunnel. The man came to them as they sat nervously in the site office, and he was almost unrecognisable from his former self, bright-eyed and rosy cheeked.

'That tiny pipe, that little bit of nothingness in a great clunk of engine. You were right, lass, you were absolutely right, and I don't care if I tell the world about it, so help me. We'll be through to them in twenty minutes max – we can hear them knocking – and we'll be just about in time; another hour or so and some of those lads would have suffocated; we can hardly hear them as it is.'

What followed, the interviews and pictures in the paper, the curiosity and interest shown around her at school, passed by Millie in a kind of blur for the next few weeks. But at the end of it, there were two very solid and cherished realities to enjoy; one, the polite and gracious departure from Roz Cooper and the dismantling of the official bedroom, with a few of the sexier pictures kept for old times' sake, and two, the real offer of an apprenticeship on a very respectable wage, in black and white and watertight as they come, as soon as she arrived at the necessary sixteen years old. The foreman, whose name was Andy, advised her to keep the press cuttings to show any scornful boys.

'Melissa of the tunnels', Dad said. 'Well done, Millie'.

She treasured the words.

THE HIGH DIVE

I am sitting in the modernist splendour of the Schwimm-und-sprung Halle im Europasportpark in Berlin, and I am one member of a crowd hushed to complete silence. We are all arrested and transfixed by an almost naked twenty year old man standing at the very edge of a high diving board.

He is what a medical friend of mine would describe as a 'perfect specimen', and I can see from the expressions of some of the watching crowd, and not just the women, that their interest in him isn't necessarily just about competitive diving.

He doesn't keep us waiting long. His fierce concentration and perfect immobility suddenly explode into action. Leaping upwards from the board, he completes a sequence of movements which very few people would consider possible for any human being to achieve in a few seconds, and then forms himself into a perfect arrow shape to enter the water.

The crowd here have already seen many dives, but they are amazed nonetheless. Long before the judges have announced their marks, everyone knows that we have just seen this Englishman retain the diving championship of Europe.

I don't know the technicalities of diving; the commentators

talk about levels of difficulty, twists, turns, sub-turns, somersaults etc., and most of it is gobbedegook to me. Nevertheless, what has just happened awakes a real pride in me, and a kind of logically absurd sense of possession. The boy who's just dived – and I still can't stop myself thinking of him as a boy – is called Dan Knowles, and he's my nephew.

The judges do what everyone expects them to do, and the hubbub grows louder. I need to get down to a certain meeting point very quickly now, but just as I start, I catch sight of a young Canadian called Brad Lovell, standing at the back of the pool beside the corridor leading down to the changing rooms. Lovell is himself an international sporting star, a sprint swimmer, and as he is Canadian and ineligible for this tournament, the widespread rumour that he is soon to be Dan's civil partner has been fed still further. On this occasion, the rumours are true. I know about the media contingents hovering around Dan, and the problems he and Brad could have getting out of this place.

Which is where I come in. I am variously called events manager, PR man, fixit merchant, whatever. Dan's mother, my dear sister Ellen, once described me to my face as a 'roadie'. She is now a head teacher, and her husband Mike boss of a sports centre; they both arrived in these 'steady, properly waged jobs', as Ellen would once have cuttingly described them as to me, by dint of 'hard work, year on year'. I managed a band's national tour, working for an agency at that time – their usual guy fell suddenly ill. I winged it with truculent locals, incompetent security managers, hacks and photographers who'd stop at nothing. 'Bits and pieces stuff, Geoff', said Ellen, or Mike, or both together. Then another band's management company asked me to handle their tour. Then another. Then a studio wanted me to look after their big name star when she came over for the BAFTAs. It mushroomed, and Ellen and Mike's tone towards their errant relative changed – not overnight, but noticeably.

Two happenings then caused them to actually ask for my services. Firstly, their remarkable son Danny became an international diving star, with the usual security issues which being in that league involve. Then, several months after his sixteenth birthday, Danny told them he was gay. I'd had a long and difficult day sorting out legal tour stuff when the call came at about half past seven. Ellie didn't bother with any routine civilities.

'He's just come in from training, with a young diver who's competing near here, and told us he's gay, Geoff. Just like that'.

'Yes, I know'.

'You know what?'

'I know he's gay'.

My sister has the gift, if it is a gift, of being able to get an entire tantrum into a single word.

'HOW?'

I reminded her of when Danny, aged fifteen, had asked me if he could join a tour of a band he thought were great at the time. He wanted to see a gig or two from the wings rather than buried in the crowd. She remembered.

'You said that he would have to do as he's told, which I thought was pretty rich, coming from you. Anyway, go on'.

I watched Danny watching the band. They had a beautiful, charismatic lead singer called Josie Summers, and almost everyone's attention was on her. But not Danny's. He was watching the lead guitar, Mel, lean and good looking, as much as I could judge about it.

One thing he had to do as he was told about was staying in a safe hotel with a room next to mine. He wasn't going walkabout on late night city streets on my watch.

We were on my room balcony talking about the gig. The way he'd looked at that guitarist worried me. If he was gay, certain things needed to happen. It wasn't about disapproval; his sexuality was and is his affair. I don't have any moral wiggle room; my love life has consisted of one night stands or short-lived affairs, and still does, what there is of it.

'Uncle Geoff', he said, in that tone kids use which lets you know something is coming down the line, 'would you mind if I asked you a very personal question?'

I grinned at him, hoping this was just banter. Daddy I wasn't, but kids do feature quite a lot in my business.

'You can ask it, Danny boy, though I'm not guaranteeing I'll answer it'.

'Are you gay?'

The pleading look on his face told me it wasn't just about curiosity.

'No, Dan, I'm not. I know your mum and dad have never invited me and partner to dinner, and that's mainly because I don't tend to knock around with the type of women I could take to dinner with your mother, and don't tell me you don't know what I mean. I've seen the fan messages you're getting. You wouldn't go short, would you?'

His eyes, to my intense distress, suddenly filled with tears.

'Not many are from boys', he said, very quietly.

'So I knew then', I said to his mother while trying to keep my eyes open. 'But he swore me to silence; he wanted to tell you and Mike himself, in his own time and his own way. And he just has'.

What came out of it wasn't quite what I expected. I became his minder.

'You know much more about this world than we do, Geoff', said his dad.

'Oh, O.K. I think I know what you mean, Mike'.

'Ellen and I have to work long hours and we can't keep getting time off. Nor would we know the best ways to protect him if we did. We're asking for your professional services, Mike, and we'll see to it you're not out of pocket'.

I decided not to be offended. That's how I've managed with Mike over the years.

'Don't worry about that. He's family. If I need whatever, I'll tell you, but it'll be mate's rates, for sure'.

I drift past the big doors where they seal off the competitors' area. The media pack are shuffling around, looking for any way to get in, even though they know perfectly well they'll be kicked straight out again if they do. I know the security chief here, Konrad Schenauer, half-German, half-Pole, as clued up as it's possible to be, and he's arranged a top grade pass for me. Through the main door, I divert to my right to a corridor only the security guys and their clients know about. I wait by an exit going straight out on to a side street.

It takes nearly half an hour, but checking situations are as they should be needs whatever time it takes. In any case, Dan will need to do poolside interviews and get changed.

Eventually, I see him and Brad hurrying towards me. Mitch, their trainer, enormous as he is, looks worried as usual.

'Geoff, thanks', he says. 'They're all over the place. The security guys said they even tried to climb the walls of the changing room'.

I can quite believe it. Nothing anyone could tell me about the lengths the media pack will go to would surprise me.

'O.K., Mitch, thanks to you. And congratulations. It's all arranged, courtesy of Konrad'.

Dan and Brad look dazed; all this stuff still spooks them occasionally. Through a side access door and we're on a Berlin street for just long enough to cross the pavement and get into a taxi with shaded windows. Even then, a guy with a camera is starting to move towards us as the taxi pulls away, fortunately in the opposite direction.

We have a suite each in a hotel slightly out of the city centre in relatively peaceful upmarket Charlottenburg. Dan and Brad collapse gratefully on to the enormous central sofa. I know when not to hang about; I know which question Dan wants to pop, and how anxious he has been to be able to pop it somewhere private enough for it to be popped properly.

'O.K., lads', I say. 'I need a drink, and you need a bit of peace, I dare say. You know my number, Dan. I'll be in 265, down the corridor.'

A couple of stiff drinks in a luxurious and quiet setting eases the nerves and the tiredness. In the restful silence, I remember Dan in a London apartment just a couple of weeks ago.

'If I win, I will definitely ask him, Geoff'. The uncle became redundant round about seventeen. 'If it's silver, and certainly if it's bronze, I'll be too pissed off to do it right, and I want to do it right'.

The light blue eyes are full on to me, and I can see the boy is finally gone. An odd sort of mixture of regret and relief washes over me.

'I remember the first time I ever stepped out on to a high board', he says. 'I was thirteen. Mitch was watching me from the ladder and he'd just nodded to someone below, so they were keeping a careful eye on me from both places. I was really, really terrified; it seemed like plunging into a miniature world below, a death jump, where you'd hit the water so hard, you'd never survive'.

'But you did it'.

'Yes. It was a simple practice dive anyway, but Mitch let me take my time, standing there, right on the ladder'. He laughed, briefly. 'But he was getting a bit restless, bored, whatever, I could read him well enough by then. So I ticked off everything he'd said in my head, and I jumped. Such a moment, Geoff. Neatly into the water, and a sudden feeling of real triumph, almost ecstasy'.

'And asking Brad, it's going to be like that?'

'It is if he says yes. I've had some tell me I'm crazy, you know. Play around for a few more years. Come out and enjoy it for a while. Play the field, see what's there. But I'm in love, Geoff, you know? And, when it comes to it, Brad and me are not boys any more. We've been all round the world, six years of it. I didn't ask for it to happen to me, but it has'.

'I don't doubt it, Dan', I said, thinking have I ever been in love with anyone at any time. Then I remembered a promise.

'Dan', I said, 'tell your mother first. Whatever Brad says, before you call through to me, tell your mother. She talks to me a lot and sometimes more than I like. But I don't want her to stop altogether. Your mum first, Dan'.

I wake up from my doze and go to stare out over Berlin, which, from way up here, is beautiful in an unexpectedly serene way. My phone sounds.

'It's yes, Uncle'.

Tears in his voice.

'It's yes. I plunged, Geoff. I was terrified again, thinking of the papers, the social media stuff. But I did it anyway; biggest dive of my life'.

'Good on you, Dan. Did you tell your mother?'

'Yes'.

'Was she pleased?'

'I think so. I'm never quite sure with Mum, you know what I mean?'

'Oh, yes, I know what you mean. Are we doing champers?'

Murmurs off stage. Brad, very loud, very happy.

'We sure as hell are, Uncle Main Man! Get your ass down here!'

'I think that's Canadian for yes, Geoff', says Dan, deadpan like he does these days.

Phone off, and I wash my soppy sod face before heading down the corridor.

PARIS BY NIGHT

Elaine watched the Cathedral of Notre Dame drift by in all its floodlit glory. At this moment, in this place, she felt a quality of quiet, unobtrusive happiness which she had rarely experienced before. Glancing across at Paul, she could see that he was not experiencing the same feelings; he seemed nervous, the cool green eyes for once quite liquid, almost frightened, their animation all the more noticeable in the subdued light of the big cruising boat, with its dark velvet and polished wood framed against the passing panorama of Paris.

'The day might come when I have a bad meal in Paris', she said softly. 'But it hasn't yet'.

'No'. Paul appeared grateful for something to be enthusiastic about. 'No, it's superb'.

He grinned at her, on this occasion a flashing, slightly mischievous expression which came and went like a light bulb. He was doing his best, but she knew the food was proving a strain in spite of its quality, and she was ninety per cent sure she knew why. The Paris weekend had been Paul's idea, including the Seine dinner cruise, a birthday treat for her. He wanted to propose; she had suspected it from the first suggestion of this trip, and now she was sure of it.

For weeks now they had been skirting round the subject, exchanging rueful stories about the pressures coming from both sets of parents, while at the same time she had to make abundantly clear that she would not give up her own flat, her own life, for anything less than the whole, proper, formal arrangement. She'd worked hard to qualify as a languages teacher and her target in the future was to move from secondary schools into higher education; none of that was going to go for any ad hoc see how it goes arrangements. She had seen the varied fates of friends, both male and female, in transitory relationships falling painfully apart or ill-considered incompatible marriages. The fact that she loved Paul, and she did, made her even more determined that things should be thoroughly and carefully done, for his sake as well as hers. They had now known each other for almost three years, and they needed to move on or risk just fading away from each other.

'Of course, Paris is familiar enough to you, I know', Paul said. 'But there are always new ways to explore it'. Another grin, and her heart went out to him. Paul always thought carefully about how best to go about everything he did, and she suspected he'd chosen the end of the meal and the romantic Paris night to do the deed. Even if his expensive food turned to ashes in his mouth, that's the way he was going to do it.

'I've never seen it quite like this before. A daytime trip, yes, but this – well, it's marvellous, Paul. Such a beautiful idea. Thank you'.

He reached a hand across to her and she held it closely. For a moment, she thought the proposal was going to come there and then. But no; he turned to one side, distracted by the elegance of the Louvre with its glass pyramid just visible behind the much older façade.

She remembered his profile in the university pool, the first time they'd ever spoken to each other. She'd only vaguely noticed him before, a clean cut young man, tall with carefully groomed straight black hair, something of the grown up boy next door. But she'd risen out of the water to see him sitting there on the side of the pool, no more than five feet away; he was watching his friends fool about at the other end. His distraction enabled her to see and enjoy the vital and perfectly sculptured figure of him.

Some instinct caused him to turn and she got a full on grin in her direction. After that, talking was easy.

And it had lasted ever since, surviving, to her surprise, through their remaining university years and even into establishing themselves in careers, she into teaching and he into the managing side of the sports centres he liked so much.

She'd been faithful to him all the way, convinced that he was the one for her, now that the relationship had survived not only the hothouse atmosphere of university but also the difficult early professional years. Her doubts, the chaos and contradictions of her younger mind, were ebbing away. In some ways, Paris, the scene of her present happiness, was also the background to her past distress.

And her heart suddenly accelerated to a drum beat when, just as she was remembering her Paris past, she found herself staring at the living embodiment of it – Alain Durand himself.

She checked herself, told herself not to be foolish; simply thinking about that insane two months with Durand in this highly charged atmosphere had made her imagine him there. But she looked again, and she knew she was not wrong. There was a very characteristic shape to Alain Durand's head and shoulders, the way he held his head high and unmoving, suggesting arrogance and a little condescension in his manner, even as he nodded agreement with his companion, a French woman of a similar age to himself. She saw Paul's head beginning to turn in the direction of her eyes and coughed furiously – anything to bring his eyes back to her, to prevent losing the mood of the evening.

'I'm sorry, Paul – something went down the wrong way. Forgive me for a moment'.

She headed away down the short staircase near them to an elaborate cloakroom full of mirrors, flowers and colours, a place for feeling cosseted and affluent rather than shaken by returning ghosts from a girlish past. What a contrast, she thought, facing the mirror critically, her plain blue eclipsed by the grandeur around her, confusion and uncertainty hijacking the promise of her evening.

Alain Durand had been a lecturer at the Sorbonne when she did her gap year. It hadn't been an easy time; after such a success at A level, she'd become complacent and underestimated how difficult it would be to deal with spoken French day in and day out. She felt out of her depth in more ways than one. Paris by day she could deal with, a whirlwind of student crowds and hectic university classes, fuelled with snatched café baguettes and sandwiches which were generally all she had the time and money for. Paris by night intimidated and puzzled her, a sophisticated world seemingly full of clever, sometimes cynical, people, cool and knowledgeable enough to find their way through complicated menus and wine lists. And she became increasingly conscious of an accompanying darkness in herself, her confidence ebbing away frighteningly into a kind of slow, slipping degeneration.

She realised that to come to terms with Paris by night and understand French life better, she needed a well-informed teacher, and she took the initiative with Durand, trusting him and herself not to let things go beyond friendship. Durand himself, benign but distant, was still, in his late twenties, holding himself back from permanent commitment. He took her at her word and they spent three evenings in restaurants while he discussed the menus and gave her an immense amount of useful information on the whole subject of Paris by night, including advice on where, what and who to avoid. On the fourth meeting, her judgement clouded by one glass of wine too many, she tried to move the relationship from friendship to romance. Durand shied away like a startled mustang, and the next day it became very clear that, as far as he was concerned, they were to be lecturer and student and no more, Durand explaining, with his own very individual mixture of humility and condescension, that he had only recently concluded a long relationship, or more accurately had it concluded for him, and he had no wish to embark upon another as yet.

She had been devastated and furiously angry at the exposure of her gauche girlishness, being made to look foolish even as she attempted to understand the worldliness of Paris, all her stereotypes about the insatiable appetites of Frenchmen rebounding on her. Now she stared into the huge mirror with its golden surround, on the verge of returning to a probable proposal of marriage. Mirror examinations are not always about vanity, she thought, seeking to reassure herself that the face looking back at her was now a young woman's with a reasonably well developed ability to judge character.

Fortunately, there were only weeks to the end of the gap year when Durand made his so patient and so hurtful little speech. Back on home territory, she had found her feet again and met Paul within a year of starting university.

She saw with sudden clarity the nature of her anxiety now, that the approaching marriage would be Paris by night all over again, but even more so, because this time she would not be able to fly home and put the pieces back together again. This time, if she once again found herself out of her depth and the cynics and sophisticates were right about the negative side of married life, she would be stuck with it or forced into an even more painful and complicated situation. She knew Paul wanted children from their discussions about it, and that was one more area covered in a mist of inexperience, where her knowledge might yet fall far short of the reality, another Paris by night lurking in the shadows.

Sympathy for the nervous, apprehensive man waiting for her in the restaurant forced her to head back to him. As she closed the cloakroom door and stepped into the corridor, Alain Durand was suddenly only five feet away, coming out of the adjacent door. A few seconds' wild panic again, but Durand clearly no longer recognised her as he passed and climbed the stairs with a quick glance and a civil nod. She made to follow him, and saw him suddenly freeze half way up the stairs, seemingly caught in a moment of indecision.

However, he did not look back and resumed the stairs after a few seconds.

Paul was more anxious than ever, rising from his seat and almost coming to meet her; she gathered what confidence she could and managed a fair attempt at the radiant smile. She resolved that the evening would not be derailed without a fight. By the time they'd reached the coffee, he seemed reassured and a small, deep blue box appeared from one of his jacket pockets. Elaine glanced across at Durand; now he had remembered, and a warm smile of recognition pleased and disconcerted her at the same time. The head waiter, a tall, elegant middle-aged man with an infectious smile, was watching from the saloon's central table; one or two of the other waiters seemed to be glancing in their direction occasionally. She turned to face Paul, who was flushed with wine and nerves.

'Elaine, you must know how I feel and I don't suppose this will come as any kind of a surprise. I know you want us to do this properly, and I do too, so much. You're everything to me, Elaine, absolutely everything. Will you please, please, marry me?'

She leaned forward; she delayed for a moment, as if trembling on a cliff edge, then the depth of her love for this man broke spectacularly over her like a wave, and she saw that nothing, **nothing** worth doing could be predicted or totally understood beforehand and if it could, how worthwhile would it be in any case?

Yes, without a doubt Paris by night had its dark corners, its shadows hiding behind the candles and romance, its traps for the unwary, but it also had almost everything she wanted from life and there was no gain without risk and adventure. Perhaps risk and adventure was what it was all about. She'd decided long ago that she would not put him off with evasive talk about time to think; here he waited before her, his beautiful eyes glistening, his cheeks glowing softly in the gentle light, his mouth tight and expectant. No diplomacy, no teasing, no ambiguities.

'Yes, Paul, yes I will, with all my heart'. They clasped hands in the middle of the table. The head waiter, who had seemed to be rocketing backwards and forwards on some spring attached to the table, could no longer contain himself and shot forward.

'Alors, Monsieur, elle a dit 'oui', n'est-ce-pas?'

Paul did what he usually did when confronted with French, look amiably mystified; Elaine made the customary intervention.

'He's asking you whether I said yes, darling'.

Paul managed to look baffled, then indignant, and then hugely amused, a great wide grin of delight and relief spreading over his face 'Yes, Monsieur, she did, she said 'yes', I mean 'oui'!'

Handshakes all round and a French both cheeks kiss from the head waiter; a short, embarrassing but warm round of applause from their fellow diners, including Alain Durand, his chair actually momentarily turned towards her, and his companion smiling even as her eyes narrowed slightly.

Later, as Paul got into conversation with a nearby English couple, she excused herself to take a little air. She walked out to the gallery at the rear of the boat, her breath catching at the cool of the night. Passing slowly by like a beautifully lit white marble boat beside them was the Basilica of Sacre Couer on Montmartre Hill; Paris by night awesome, mysterious, fascinating as ever.

A voice spoke her name in that careful, articulate way the French did, and she turned to see Alain Durand standing beside her.

'I look at that lovely profile and think I was very unfair to you those years ago; so cold, so withdrawn. My life was very mixed up at that time. But don't ever think I wasn't tempted; you are wonderful, and I wish you all the happiness in the world'.

'Thank you, Alain'. She heard herself saying the words so easily as she stared at the glistening waters of the Seine and remembered another time of looking into this river, when, for a brief but terrifying passage of time, she was seriously considering drastic action to remove or at least divert the pain she was feeling.

'And did you find what you were looking for, Alain?'

His eyes melted towards her.

'Francoise is my wife. She is remarkable, and amazingly, was prepared to have me.

I have never been so happy'.

A few minutes later, they walked back to their seats, and she felt Durand's eyes following her in farewell. Paul reached across to take her hand. At that moment, a long, sleek cruising boat passed them in the opposite direction. Several people were waving towards them. They each lifted their free hand and waved happily back.